The Collected Supernatural and Weird Fiction of Elia W. Peattie

The Collected Supernatural and Weird Fiction of Elia W. Peattie

Twenty-Two Short Stories
of the Strange and Unusual

Elia W. Peattie

LEONAUR

The Collected
Supernatural and Weird
Fiction of
Elia W. Peattie
Twenty-Two Short Stories of the Strange and Unusual
by Elia W. Peattie

FIRST EDITION

Leonaur is an imprint
of Oakpast Ltd

ISBN: 978-1-78282-154-0 (hardcover)
ISBN:978-1-78282-155-7 (softcover)

http://www.leonaur.com

Contents

A Child of the Rain

It was the night that Mona Meeks, the dressmaker, told him she didn't love him. He couldn't believe it at first, because he had so long been accustomed to the idea that she did, and no matter how rough the weather or how irascible the passengers, he felt a song in his heart as he punched transfers, and rang his bell punch, and signalled the driver when to let people off and on.

Now, suddenly, with no reason except a woman's, she had changed her mind. He dropped in to see her at five o'clock, just before time for the night shift, and to give her two red apples he had been saving for her. She looked at the apples as if they were invisible and she could not see them, and standing in her disorderly little dressmaking parlour, with its cuttings and scraps and litter of fabrics, she said:

"It is no use, John. I shall have to work here like this all my life—work here alone. For I don't love you, John. No, I don't. I thought I did, but it is a mistake."

"You mean it?" asked John, bringing up the words in a great gasp.

"Yes," she said, white and trembling and putting out her hands as if to beg for his mercy. And then—big, lumbering fool—he turned around and strode down the stairs and stood at the corner in the beating rain waiting for his car. It came along at length, spluttering on the wet rails and spitting out blue fire, and he took his shift after a gruff "Goodnight" to Johnson, the man he relieved.

He was glad the rain was bitter cold and drove in his face

fiercely. He rejoiced at the cruelty of the wind, and when it hustled pedestrians before it, lashing them, twisting their clothes, and threatening their equilibrium, he felt amused. He was pleased at the chill in his bones and at the hunger that tortured him. At least, at first he thought it was hunger till he remembered that he had just eaten.

The hours passed confusedly. He had no consciousness of time. But it must have been late,—near midnight,—judging by the fact that there were few persons visible anywhere in the black storm, when he noticed a little figure sitting at the far end of the car. He had not seen the child when she got on, but all was so curious and wild to him that evening—he himself seemed to himself the most curious and the wildest of all things—that it was not surprising that he should not have observed the little creature.

She was wrapped in a coat so much too large that it had become frayed at the bottom from dragging on the pavement. Her hair hung in unkempt stringiness about her bent shoulders, and her feet were covered with old arctics, many sizes too big, from which the soles hung loose.

Beside the little figure was a chest of dark wood, with curiously wrought hasps. From this depended a stout strap by which it could be carried over the shoulders. John Billings stared in, fascinated by the poor little thing with its head sadly drooping upon its breast, its thin blue hands relaxed upon its lap, and its whole attitude so suggestive of hunger, loneliness, and fatigue, that he made up his mind he would collect no fare from it.

"It will need its nickel for breakfast," he said to himself. "The company can stand this for once. Or, come to think of it, I might celebrate my hard luck. Here's to the brotherhood of failures!" And he took a nickel from one pocket of his great-coat and dropped it in another, ringing his bell punch to record the transfer.

The car plunged along in the darkness, and the rain beat more viciously than ever in his face. The night was full of the rushing sound of the storm. Owing to some change of temperature the glass of the car became obscured so that the young conductor could no longer see the little figure distinctly, and he grew anxious about the child.

"I wonder if it's all right," he said to himself. "I never saw living creature sit so still."

He opened the car door, intending to speak with the child, but just then something went wrong with the lights. There was a blue and green flickering, then darkness, a sudden halting of the car, and a great sweep of wind and rain in at the door. When, after a moment, light and motion reasserted themselves, and Billings had got the door together, he turned to look at the little passenger. But the car was empty.

It was a fact. There was no child there—not even moisture on the seat where she had been sitting.

"Bill," said he, going to the front door and addressing the driver, "what became of that little kid in the old cloak?"

"I didn't see no kid," said Bill, crossly. "For Gawd's sake, close the door, John, and git that draught off my back."

"Draught!" said John, indignantly, "where's the draught?"

"You've left the hind door open," growled Bill, and John saw him shivering as a blast struck him and ruffled the fur on his bear-skin coat. But the door was not open, and yet John had to admit to himself that the car seemed filled with wind and a strange coldness.

However, it didn't matter. Nothing mattered! Still, it was as well no doubt to look under the seats just to make sure no little crouching figure was there, and so he did. But there was nothing. In fact, John said to himself, he seemed to be getting expert in finding nothing where there ought to be something.

He might have stayed in the car, for there was no likelihood of more passengers that evening, but somehow he preferred going out where the rain could drench him and the wind pommel him. How horribly tired he was! If there were only some still place away from the blare of the city where a man could lie down and listen to the sound of the sea or the storm—or if one could grow suddenly old and get through with the bother of living—or if—

The car gave a sudden lurch as it rounded a curve, and for a moment it seemed to be a mere chance whether Conductor Billings would stay on his platform or go off under those fire-spitting wheels. He caught instinctively at his brake, saved himself, and stood still for a moment, panting.

"I must have dozed," he said to himself.

Just then, dimly, through the blurred window, he saw again the little figure of the child, its head on its breast as before, its blue hands lying in its lap and the curious box beside it. John Billings felt a coldness beyond the coldness of the night run through his blood. Then, with a half-stifled cry, he threw back the door, and made a desperate spring at the corner where the eerie thing sat.

And he touched the green carpeting on the seat, which was quite dry and warm, as if no dripping, miserable little wretch had ever crouched there.

He rushed to the front door.

"Bill," he roared, "I want to know about that kid."

"What kid?"

"The same kid! The wet one with the old coat and the box with iron hasps! The one that's been sitting here in the car!"

Bill turned his surly face to confront the young conductor.

"You've been drinking, you fool," said he. "Fust thing you know you'll be reported."

The conductor said not a word. He went slowly and weakly back to his post and stood there the rest of the way leaning against the end of the car for support. Once or twice he muttered:

"The poor little brat!" And again he said, "So you didn't love me after all!"

He never knew how he reached home, but he sank to sleep as dying men sink to death. All the same, being a hearty young man, he was on duty again next day but one, and again the night was rainy and cold.

It was the last run, and the car was spinning along at its limit, when there came a sudden soft shock. John Billings knew what that meant. He had felt something of the kind once before. He turned sick for a moment, and held on to the brake. Then he summoned his courage and went around to the side of the car, which had stopped. Bill, the driver, was before him, and had a limp little figure in his arms, and was carrying it to the gaslight. John gave one look and cried:

"It's the same kid, Bill! The one I told you of!"

True as truth were the ragged coat dangling from the pitiful body, the little blue hands, the thin shoulders, the stringy hair, the big arctics on the feet. And in the road not far off was the curious chest of dark wood with iron hasps.

"She ran under the car deliberate!" cried Bill. "I yelled to her, but she looked at me and ran straight on!"

He was white in spite of his weather-beaten skin.

"I guess you wasn't drunk last night after all, John," said he.

"You—you are sure the kid is—is there?" gasped John.

"Not so damned sure!" said Bill.

But a few minutes later it was taken away in a patrol wagon, and with it the little box with iron hasps.

A Grammatical Ghost

There was only one possible objection to the drawing-room, and that was the occasional presence of Miss Carew; and only one possible objection to Miss Carew. And that was, that she was dead.

She had been dead twenty years, as a matter of fact and record, and to the last of her life sacredly preserved the treasures and traditions of her family, a family bound up—as it is quite unnecessary to explain to any one in good society—with all that is most venerable and heroic in the history of the Republic. Miss Carew never relaxed the proverbial hospitality of her house, even when she remained its sole representative. She continued to preside at her table with dignity and state, and to set an example of excessive modesty and gentle decorum to a generation of restless young women.

It is not likely that having lived a life of such irreproachable gentility as this, Miss Carew would have the bad taste to die in any way not pleasant to mention in fastidious society. She could be trusted to the last, not to outrage those friends who quoted her as an exemplar of propriety. She died very unobtrusively of an affection of the heart, one June morning, while trimming her rose trellis, and her lavender-coloured print was not even rumpled when she fell, nor were more than the tips of her little bronze slippers visible.

"Isn't it dreadful," said the Philadelphians, "that the property should go to a very, very distant cousin in Iowa or somewhere else on the frontier, about whom nobody knows anything at all?"

The Carew treasures were packed in boxes and sent away into the Iowa wilderness; the Carew traditions were preserved by the Historical Society; the Carew property, standing in one of the most umbrageous and aristocratic suburbs of Philadelphia, was rented to all manner of folk—anybody who had money enough to pay the rental—and society entered its doors no more.

But at last, after twenty years, and when all save the oldest Philadelphians had forgotten Miss Lydia Carew, the very, very distant cousin appeared. He was quite in the prime of life, and so agreeable and unassuming that nothing could be urged against him save his patronymic, which, being Boggs, did not commend itself to the euphemists. With him were two maiden sisters, ladies of excellent taste and manners, who restored the Carew china to its ancient cabinets, and replaced the Carew pictures upon the walls, with additions not out of keeping with the elegance of these heirlooms. Society, with a magnanimity almost dramatic, overlooked the name of Boggs—and called.

All was well. At least, to an outsider all seemed to be well. But, in truth, there was a certain distress in the old mansion, and in the hearts of the well-behaved Misses Boggs. It came about most unexpectedly. The sisters had been sitting upstairs, looking out at the beautiful grounds of the old place, and marvelling at the violets, which lifted their heads from every possible cranny about the house, and talking over the cordiality which they had been receiving by those upon whom they had no claim, and they were filled with amiable satisfaction. Life looked attractive. They had often been grateful to Miss Lydia Carew for leaving their brother her fortune. Now they felt even more grateful to her. She had left them a Social Position—one, which even after twenty years of desuetude, was fit for use.

They descended the stairs together, with arms clasped about each other's waists, and as they did so presented a placid and pleasing sight. They entered their drawing-room with the intention of brewing a cup of tea, and drinking it in calm sociability in the twilight. But as they entered the room they became aware of the presence of a lady, who was already seated at their tea-table, regarding their old Wedgewood with the air of a connoisseur.

There were a number of peculiarities about this intruder. To begin with, she was hatless, quite as if she were a *habitué*; of the house, and was costumed in a prim lilac-coloured lawn of the style of two decades past. But a greater peculiarity was the resemblance this lady bore to a faded daguerrotype. If looked at one way, she was perfectly discernible; if looked at another, she went out in a sort of blur. Notwithstanding this comparative invisibility, she exhaled a delicate perfume of sweet lavender, very pleasing to the nostrils of the Misses Boggs, who stood looking at her in gentle and unprotesting surprise.

"I beg your pardon," began Miss Prudence, the younger of the Misses Boggs, "but—"

But at this moment the daguerrotype became a blur, and Miss Prudence found herself addressing space. The Misses Boggs were irritated. They had never encountered any mysteries in Iowa. They began an impatient search behind doors and *portières*, and even under sofas, though it was quite absurd to suppose that a lady recognizing the merits of the Carew Wedgewood would so far forget herself as to crawl under a sofa.

When they had given up all hope of discovering the intruder, they saw her standing at the far end of the drawing-room critically examining a water-colour marine. The elder Miss Boggs started toward her with stern decision, but the little daguerrotype turned with a shadowy smile, became a blur and an imperceptibility.

Miss Boggs looked at Miss Prudence Boggs.

"If there were ghosts," she said, "this would be one."

"*If* there were ghosts," said Miss Prudence Boggs, "this would be the ghost of Lydia Carew."

The twilight was settling into blackness, and Miss Boggs nervously lit the gas while Miss Prudence ran for other tea-cups, preferring, for reasons superfluous to mention, not to drink out of the Carew china that evening.

The next day, on taking up her embroidery frame, Miss Boggs found a number of old-fashioned cross-stitches added to her Kensington. Prudence, she knew, would never have degraded herself by taking a cross-stitch, and the parlour-maid was above taking such a liberty. Miss Boggs mentioned the incident that night at a dinner given by an ancient friend of the Carews.

"Oh, that's the work of Lydia Carew, without a doubt!" cried the hostess. "She visits every new family that moves to the house, but she never remains more than a week or two with anyone."

"It must be that she disapproves of them," suggested Miss Boggs.

"I think that's it," said the hostess. "She doesn't like their china, or their fiction."

"I hope she'll disapprove of us," added Miss Prudence.

The hostess belonged to a very old Philadelphian family, and she shook her head.

"I should say it was a compliment for even the ghost of Miss Lydia Carew to approve of one," she said severely.

The next morning, when the sisters entered their drawing-room there were numerous evidences of an occupant during their absence. The sofa pillows had been rearranged so that the effect of their grouping was less bizarre than that favoured by the Western women; a horrid little Buddhist idol with its eyes fixed on its abdomen, had been chastely hidden behind a Dresden shepherdess, as unfit for the scrutiny of polite eyes; and on the table where Miss Prudence did work in water colours, after the fashion of the impressionists, lay a prim and impossible composition representing a moss-rose and a number of heartsease, coloured with that caution which modest spinster artists instinctively exercise.

"Oh, there's no doubt it's the work of Miss Lydia Carew," said Miss Prudence, contemptuously. "There's no mistaking the drawing of that rigid little rose. Don't you remember those wreaths and bouquets framed, among the pictures we got when the Carew pictures were sent to us? I gave some of them to an orphan asylum and burned up the rest."

"Hush!" cried Miss Boggs, involuntarily. "If she heard you, it would hurt her feelings terribly. Of course, I mean—" and she blushed. "It might hurt her feelings—but how perfectly ridiculous! It's impossible!"

Miss Prudence held up the sketch of the moss-rose.

"*That* may be impossible in an artistic sense, but it is a palpable thing."

"Bosh!" cried Miss Boggs.

"But," protested Miss Prudence, "how do you explain it?"

"I don't," said Miss Boggs, and left the room.

That evening the sisters made a point of being in the drawing-room before the dusk came on, and of lighting the gas at the first hint of twilight. They didn't believe in Miss Lydia Carew—but still they meant to be beforehand with her. They talked with unwonted vivacity and in a louder tone than was their custom. But as they drank their tea even their utmost verbosity could not make them oblivious to the fact that the perfume of sweet lavender was stealing insidiously through the room. They tacitly refused to recognize this odour and all that it indicated, when suddenly, with a sharp crash, one of the old Carew tea-cups fell from the tea-table to the floor and was broken. The disaster was followed by what sounded like a sigh of pain and dismay.

"I didn't suppose Miss Lydia Carew would ever be as awkward as that," cried the younger Miss Boggs, petulantly.

"Prudence," said her sister with a stern accent, "please try not to be a fool. You brushed the cup off with the sleeve of your dress."

"Your theory wouldn't be so bad," said Miss Prudence, half laughing and half crying, "if there were any sleeves to my dress, but, as you see, there aren't," and then Miss Prudence had something as near hysterics as a healthy young woman from the West can have.

"I wouldn't think such a perfect lady as Lydia Carew," she ejaculated between her sobs, "would make herself so disagreeable! You may talk about good-breeding all you please, but I call such intrusion exceedingly bad taste. I have a horrible idea that she likes us and means to stay with us. She left those other people because she did not approve of their habits or their grammar. It would be just our luck to please her."

"Well, I like your egotism," said Miss Boggs.

However, the view Miss Prudence took of the case appeared to be the right one. Time went by and Miss Lydia Carew still remained. When the ladies entered their drawing-room they would see the little lady-like daguerrotype revolving itself into a blur before one of the family portraits. Or they noticed that the yellow sofa cushion, toward which she appeared to feel a peculiar antipathy, had been dropped behind the sofa upon the floor, or that one of Jane Austen's novels, which none of the family ever read, had been removed from the book shelves and left open upon the table.

"I cannot become reconciled to it," complained Miss Boggs to Miss Prudence. "I wish we had remained in Iowa where we belong. Of course I don't believe in the thing! No sensible person would. But still I cannot become reconciled."

But their liberation was to come, and in a most unexpected manner.

A relative by marriage visited them from the West. He was a friendly man and had much to say, so he talked all through dinner, and afterward followed the ladies to the drawing-room to finish his gossip. The gas in the room was turned very low, and as they entered Miss Prudence caught sight of Miss Carew, in company attire, sitting in upright propriety in a stiff-backed chair at the extremity of the apartment.

Miss Prudence had a sudden idea.

"We will not turn up the gas," she said, with an emphasis intended to convey private information to her sister. "It will be more agreeable to sit here and talk in this soft light."

Neither her brother nor the man from the West made any objection. Miss Boggs and Miss Prudence, clasping each other's hands, divided their attention between their corporeal and their incorporeal guests. Miss Boggs was confident that her sister had an idea, and was willing to await its development. As the guest from Iowa spoke, Miss Carew bent a politely attentive ear to what he said.

"Ever since Richards took sick that time," he said briskly, "it seemed like he shed all responsibility." (The Misses Boggs saw the daguerrotype put up her shadowy head with a movement of doubt and apprehension.) "The fact of the matter was, Richards didn't seem to scarcely get on the way he might have been expected to." (At this conscienceless split to the infinitive and misplacing of the preposition, Miss Carew arose trembling perceptibly.) "I saw it wasn't no use for him to count on a quick recovery—"

The Misses Boggs lost the rest of the sentence, for at the utterance of the double negative Miss Lydia Carew had flashed out, not in a blur, but with mortal haste, as when life goes out at a pistol shot!

The man from the West wondered why Miss Prudence should have cried at so pathetic a part of his story:

"Thank Goodness!"

And their brother was amazed to see Miss Boggs kiss Miss Prudence with passion and energy.

It was the end. Miss Carew returned no more.

A Lady of Yesterday

"A light wind blew from the gates of the sun," the morning she first walked down the street of the little Iowa town. Not a cloud flecked the blue; there was a humming of happy insects; a smell of rich and moist loam perfumed the air, and in the dusk of beeches and of oaks stood the quiet homes. She paused now and then, looking in the gardens, or at a group of children, then passed on, smiling in content.

Her accent was so strange, that the agent for real estate, whom she visited, asked her, twice and once again, what it was she said.

"I want," she had repeated smilingly, "an upland meadow, where clover will grow, and mignonette."

At the tea-tables that night, there was a mighty chattering. The brisk village made a mystery of this lady with the slow step, the foreign trick of speech, the long black gown, and the gentle voice. The men, concealing their curiosity in presence of the women, gratified it secretly, by sauntering to the tavern in the evening. There the keeper and his wife stood ready to convey any neighborly intelligence.

"Elizabeth Astrado" was written in the register,—a name conveying little, unaccompanied by title or by place of residence.

"She eats alone," the tavern-keeper's wife confided to their eager ears, "and asks for no service. Oh, she's a curiosity! She's got her story,—you'll see!"

In a town where every man knew every other man, and whether or not he paid his taxes on time, and what his standing was in church, and all the skeletons of his home, a stranger alien to their ways disturbed their peace of mind.

"An upland meadow where clover and mignonette will grow," she had said, and such an one she found, and planted thick with fine white clover and with mignonette. Then, while the carpenters raised her cabin at the border of the meadow, near the street, she passed among the villagers, mingling with them gently, winning their good-will, in spite of themselves.

The cabin was of unbarked maple logs, with four rooms and a rustic portico. Then all the villagers stared in very truth. They, living in their trim and ugly little homes, accounted houses of logs as the misfortune of their pioneer parents. A shed for wood, a barn for the Jersey cow, a rustic fence, tall, with a high swinging gate, completed the domain. In the front room of the cabin was a fireplace of rude brick. In the bedrooms, cots as bare and hard as a nun's, and in the kitchen the domestic necessaries; that was all. The poorest house-holder in the town would not have confessed to such scant furnishing. Yet the richest man might well have hesitated before he sent to France for hives and hives of bees, as she did, setting them up along the southern border of her meadow.

Later there came strong boxes, marked with many marks of foreign transportation lines, and the neighbor-gossips, seeing them, imagined wealth of curious furniture; but the man who carted them told his wife, who told her friend, who told her friend, that every box to the last one was placed in the dry cemented cellar, and left there in the dark.

"An' a mighty ridic'lous expense a cellar like that is, t' put under a house of that char'cter," said the man to his wife—who repeated it to her friend.

"But that ain't all," the carpenter's wife had said when she heard about it all, "Hank says there is one little room, not fit for buttery nor yet fur closit, with a window high up—well, you ken see yourself-an' a strong door. Jus' in passin' th' other day, when he was there, hangin' some shelves, he tried it, an' it was locked!"

"Well!" said the women who listened.

However, they were not unfriendly, these brisk gossips. Two of them, plucking up tardy courage, did call one afternoon. Their hostess was out among her bees, crooning to them, as it seemed, while they lighted all about her, lit on the flower in her dark hair, buzzed vivaciously about her snow-white linen gown, lighted on her long, dark hands. She came in brightly when she saw her guests, and placed chairs for them, courteously, steeped them a cup of pale and fragrant tea, and served them with little cakes. Though her manner was so quiet and so kind, the women were shy before her. She, turning to one and then the other, asked questions in her quaint way.

"You have children, have you not?"

Both of them had.

"Ah," she cried, clasping those slender hands, "but you are very fortunate! Your little ones,—what are their ages?"

They told her, she listening smilingly.

"And you nurse your little babes—you nurse them at the breast?"

The modest women blushed. They were not used to speaking with such freedom. But they confessed they did, not liking artificial means.

"No," said the lady, looking at them with a soft light in her eyes, "as you say, there is nothing like the good mother Nature. The little ones God sends should lie at the breast. 'Tis not the milk alone that they imbibe; it is the breath of life,—it is the human magnetism, the power,—how shall I say? Happy the mother who has a little babe to hold!"

They wanted to ask a question, but they dared not—wanted to ask a hundred questions. But back of the gentleness was a hauteur, and they were still.

"Tell me," she said, breaking her reverie, "of what your husbands do. Are they carpenters? Do they build houses for men, like the blessed Jesus? Or are they tillers of the soil? Do they bring fruits out of this bountiful valley?"

They answered, with a reservation of approval. "The blessed

Jesus!" It sounded like popery.

She had gone from these brief personal matters to other things.

"How very strong you people seem," she had remarked. "Both your men and your women are large and strong. You should be, being appointed to subdue a continent. Men think they choose their destinies, but indeed, good neighbors, I think not so. Men are driven by the winds of God's will. They are as much bidden to build up this valley, this storehouse for the nations, as coral insects are bidden to make the reefs with their own little bodies, dying as they build. Is it not so?"

"We are the creatures of God's will, I suppose," said one of her visitors, piously.

She had given them little confidences in return.

"I make my bread," she said, with childish pride, "pray see if you do not think it excellent!" And she cut a flaky loaf to display its whiteness. One guest summoned the bravado to inquire,—

"Then you are not used to doing housework?"

"I?" she said, with a slow smile, "I have never got used to anything,—not even living." And so she baffled them all, yet won them.

The weeks went by. Elizabeth Astrado attended to her bees, milked her cow, fed her fowls, baked, washed, and cleaned, like the simple women about her, saving that as she did it a look of ineffable content lighted up her face, and she sang for happiness. Sometimes, amid the ballads that she hummed, a strain slipped in of some great melody, which she, singing unaware, as it were, corrected, shaking her finger in self-reproval, and returning again to the ballads and the hymns. Nor was she remiss in neighborly offices; but if any were ailing, or had a festivity, she was at hand to assist, condole, or congratulate, carrying always some simple gift in her hand, appropriate to the occasion.

She had her wider charities too, for all she kept close to her home. When, one day, a story came to her of a laborer struck down with heat in putting in a culvert on the railroad, and gossip said he could not speak English, she hastened to him, caught dying words from his lips, whispered a reply, and then what seemed to be a prayer, while he held fast her hand, and sank to coma with wistful eyes upon her face. Moreover 'twas she who buried him, raising a cross above his grave, and she who planted rose-bushes about the mound.

"He spoke like an Italian," said the physician to her warily.

"And so he was," she had replied.

"A fellow-countryman of yours, no doubt?"

"Are not all men our countrymen, my friend?" she said, gently. "What are little lines drawn in the imagination of men, dividing territory, that they should divide our sympathies? The world is my country—and yours, I hope. Is it not so?"

Then there had also been a hapless pair of lovers, shamed before their community, who, desperate, impoverished, and bewildered at the war between nature and society, had been helped by her into a new part of the world. There had been a widow with many children, who had found baskets of cooked food and bundles of well-made clothing on her step. And as the days passed, with these pleasant offices, the face of the strange woman glowed with an ever-increasing content, and her dark, delicate beauty grew.

John Hartington spent his vacation at Des Moines, having a laudable desire to see something of the world before returning to his native town, with his college honors fresh upon him. Swiftest of the college runners was John Hartington, famed for his leaping too, and measuring widest at the chest and waist of all the hearty fellows at the university. His blond curls clustered above a brow almost as innocent as a child's; his frank and brave blue eyes, his free step, his mellow laugh, bespoke the perfect animal, unharmed by civilization, unperplexed by the closing century's fallacies and passions. The wholesome oak that spreads its roots deep in the generous soil, could not be more a part of nature than he. Conscientious, unimaginative, direct, sincere, industrious, he was the ideal man of his kind, and his return to town caused a flutter among the maidens which they did not even attempt to conceal. They told him all the chat, of course, and, among other things, mentioned the great sensation of the year,—the coming of the woman with her mystery, the purchase of the sunny upland, the planting it with clover and with mignonette, the building of the house of logs, the keeping of the bees, the barren rooms, the busy, silent life, the charities, the never-ending wonder of it all. And then the woman—kind, yet different from the rest, with the foreign trick of tongue, the slow, proud walk, the delicate, slight hands, the beautiful, beautiful smile, the air as of a creature from another world.

Hartington, strolling beyond the village streets, up where the sunset died in daffodil above the upland, saw the little cot of logs, and out before it, among blood-red poppies, the woman of whom he had heard. Her gown of white gleamed in that eerie radiance, glorified, her sad great eyes bent on him in magnetic scrutiny. A peace and plenitude of power came radiating from her, and reached him where he stood, suddenly, and for the first time in his careless life, struck dumb and awed. She, too, seemed suddenly abashed at this great bulk of youthful manhood, innocent and strong.

She gazed on him, and he on her, both chained with some mysterious enchantment. Yet neither spoke, and he, turning in bewilderment at last, went back to town, while she placed one hand on her lips to keep from calling him. And neither slept that night, and in the morning when she went with milking pail and stool out to the grassy field, there he stood at the bars, waiting. Again they gazed, like creatures held in thrall by some magician, till she held out her hand and said,—

"We must be friends, although we have not met. Perhaps we *are* old friends. They say there have been worlds before this one. I have not seen you in these habiliments of flesh and blood, and yet—we may be friends?"

John Hartington, used to the thin jests of the village girls, and all their simple talk, rose, nevertheless, enlightened as he was with some strange sympathy with her, to understand and answer what she said.

"I think perhaps it may be so. May I come in beside you in

the field? Give me the pail. I'll milk the cow for you."

She threw her head back and laughed like a girl from school, and he laughed too, and they shook hands. Then she sat near him while he milked, both keeping silence, save for the *p-rring* noise he made with his lips to the patient beast. Being through, she served him with a cupful of the fragrant milk; but he bade her drink first, then drank himself, and then they laughed again, as if they both had found something new and good in life.

Then she,—

"Come see how well my bees are doing."

And they went. She served him with the lucent syrup of the bees, perfumed with the mignonette,—such honey as there never was before. He sat on the broad doorstep, near the scarlet poppies, she on the grass, and then they talked—was it one golden hour—or two? Ah, well, 'twas long enough for her to learn all of his simple life, long enough for her to know that he was victor at the races at the school, that he could play the pipe, like any shepherd of the ancient days, and when he went he asked her if he might return.

"Well," laughed she, "sometimes I am lonely. Come see me— in a week."

Yet he was there that day at twilight, and he brought his silver pipe, and piped to her under the stars, and she sung ballads to him,—songs of Strephon and times when the hills were young, and flocks were fairer than they ever be these days.

"Tomorrow, and tomorrow, and tomorrow," and still the intercourse, still her dark loveliness waxing, still the weaving of the mystic spell, still happiness as primitive and as sweet as ever Eden knew.

Then came a twilight when the sweet rain fell, and on the heavy air the perfumes of the fields floated. The woman stood by the window of the cot, looking out. Tall, graceful, full of that subtle power which drew his soul; clothed in white linen, fragrant from her fields, with breath freighted with fresh milk, with eyes of flame, she was there to be adored. And he, being man of manliest type, forgot all that might have checked the words, and poured his soul out at her feet. She drew herself up like a queen, but only that she might look queenlier for his sake, and, bending, kissed his brow, and whispered back his vows.

And they were married.

The villagers pitied Hartington.

"She's more than a match for him in years—an' in some other ways, as like as not," they said. "Besides, she ain't much inclined to mention anything about her past. 'Twon't bear the tellin' probably."

As for the lovers, they laughed as they went about their honest tasks, or sat together arms encircling each at evening, now under the stars, and now before their fire of wood. They talked together of their farm, added a field for winter wheat, bought other cattle, and some horses, which they rode out over the rolling prairies side by side. He never stopped to chat about the town; she never ventured on the street without him by her side. Truth to tell, their neighbors envied them, marvelling how one could extract a heaven out of earth, and what such perfect joy could mean.

Yet, for all their prosperity, not one addition did they make to that most simple home. It stood there, with its bare necessities, made beautiful only with their love. But when the winter was most gone, he made a little cradle of hard wood, in which she placed pillows of down, and over which she hung linen curtains embroidered by her hand.

In the long evenings, by the flicker of the fire, they sat together, cheek to cheek, and looked at this little bed, singing low songs together.

"This happiness is terrible, my John," she said to him one night,—a wondrous night, when the eastern wind had flung the tassels out on all the budding trees of spring, and the air was throbbing with awakening life, and balmy puffs of breeze, and odors of the earth. "And we are growing young. Do you not think that we are very young and strong?"

He kissed her on the lips. "I know that you are beautiful," he said.

26

"Oh, we have lived at Nature's heart, you see, my love. The cattle and the fowls, the honey and the wheat, the cot-the cradle, John, and you and me! These things make happiness. They are nature. But then, you cannot understand. You have never known the artificial—"

"And you, Elizabeth?"

"John, if you wish, you shall hear all I have to tell. 'Tis a long, long, weary tale. Will you hear it now? Believe me, it will make us sad."

She grasped his arm till he shrank with pain.

"Tell what you will and when you will, Elizabeth. Perhaps, some day—when—" he pointed to the little crib.

"As you say." And so it dropped.

There came a day when Hartington, sitting upon the portico, where perfumes of the budding clover came to him, hated the humming of the happy bees, hated the rustling of the trees, hated the sight of earth.

"The child is dead," the nurse had said, "as for your wife, perhaps—" but that was all. Finally he heard the nurse's step upon the floor.

"Come," she said, motioning him. And he had gone, laid cheek against that dying cheek, whispered his love once more, saw it returned even then, in those deep eyes, and laid her back upon her pillow, dead.

He buried her among the mignonette, levelled the earth, sowed thick the seed again.

"'Tis as she wished," he said.

With his strong hands he wrenched the little crib, laid it piece by piece upon their hearth, and scattered then the sacred ashes on the wind. Then, with hard-coming breath, broke open the locked door of that room which he had never entered, thinking to find there, perhaps, some sign of that unguessable life of hers, but found there only an altar, with votive lamps before the Blessed Virgin, and lilies faded and fallen from their stems.

Then down into the cellar went he, to those boxes, with the foreign marks. And then, indeed, he found a hint of that dead life.

Gowns of velvet and of silk, such as princesses might wear, wonders of lace, yellowed with time, great cloaks of snowy fur, lustrous robes, jewels of worth,—a vast array of brilliant trumpery. Then there were books in many tongues, with rich old bindings and illuminated page, and in them written the dead woman's name,—a name of many parts, with titles of impress, and in the midst of all the name, "Elizabeth Astrado," as she said.

And that was all, or if there were more he might have learned, following trails that fell within his way, he never learned it, being content, and thankful that he had held her for a time within his arms, and looked in her great soul, which, wearying of life's sad complexities, had simplified itself, and made his love its best adornment.

A Michigan Man

A pine forest is nature's expression of solemnity and solitude. Sunlight, rivers, cascades, people, music, laughter, or dancing could not make it gay. With its unceasing reverberations and its eternal shadows, it is as awful and as holy as a cathedral.

Thirty good fellows working together by day and drinking together by night can keep up but a moody imitation of jollity. Spend twenty-five of your forty years, as Luther Dallas did, in this perennial gloom, and your soul—that which enjoys, aspires, competes—will be drugged as deep as if you had quaffed the cup of oblivion. Luther Dallas was counted one of the most experienced axe-men in the northern camps. He could fell a tree with the swift surety of an executioner, and in revenge for his many arboreal murders the woodland had taken captive his mind, captured and chained it as Prospero did Ariel.

The resounding footsteps of Progress driven on so mercilessly in this mad age could not reach his fastness. It did not concern him that men were thinking, investigating, inventing. His senses responded only to the sonorous music of the woods; a steadfast wind ringing metallic melody from the pine-tops contented him as the sound of the sea does the sailor; and dear as the odours of the ocean to the mariner were the resinous scents of the forest to him. Like a sailor, too, he had his superstitions. He had a presentiment that he was to die by one of these trees—that some day, in chopping, the tree would fall upon and crush him as it did his father the day they brought him back to the camp on a litter of pine boughs.

One day the gang boss noticed a tree that Dallas had left standing in a most unwoodmanlike manner in the section which was allotted to him.

"What in thunder is that standing there for?" he asked.

Dallas raised his eyes to the pine, towering in stern dignity a hundred feet above them.

"Well," he said, feebly, "I noticed it, but kind-a left it t' the last."

"Cut it down tomorrow," was the response.

The wind was rising, and the tree muttered savagely. Luther thought it sounded like a menace, and turned pale. No trouble has yet been found that will keep a man awake in the keen air of the pineries after he has been swinging his axe all day, but the sleep of the chopper was so broken with disturbing dreams that night that the beads gathered on his brow, and twice he cried aloud. He ate his coarse flap-jacks in the morning and escaped from the smoky shanty as soon as he could.

"It'll bring bad luck, I'm afraid," he muttered as he went to get his axe from the rack. He was as fond of his axe as a soldier of his musket, but today he shouldered it with reluctance. He felt like a man with his destiny before him. The tree stood like a sentinel. He raised his axe, once, twice, a dozen times, but could not bring himself to make a cut in the bark. He walked backward a few steps and looked up. The funereal green seemed to grow darker and darker till it became black. It was the embodiment of sorrow. Was it not shaking giant arms at him? Did it not cry out in angry challenge?

Luther did not try to laugh at his fears; he had never seen any humour in life. A gust of wind had someway crept through the dense barricade of foliage that flanked the clearing, and struck him with an icy chill. He looked at the sky: the day was advancing rapidly. He went at his work with an energy as determined as despair. The axe in his practiced hand made clean straight cuts in the trunk, now on this side, now on that. His task was not an easy one, but he finished it with wonderful expedition. After the chopping was finished, the tree stood firm a moment; then, as the tensely strained fibres began a weird moaning, he sprang aside, and stood waiting. In the distance he saw two men hewing a log. The axe-man sent them a shout and threw up his arms for them to look.

The tree stood out clear and beautiful against the gray sky; the men ceased their work and watched it. The vibrations became more violent, and the sounds they produced grew louder and louder till they reached a shrill wild cry. There came a pause; then a deep shuddering groan. The topmost branches began to move slowly, the whole stately bulk swayed, and then shot toward the ground. The gigantic trunk bounded from the stump, recoiled like a cannon, crashed down, and lay conquered, with a roar as of an earthquake, in a cloud of flying twigs and chips.

When the dust had cleared away, the men at the log on the outside of the clearing could not see Luther. They ran to the spot, and found him lying on the ground with his chest crushed in. His fearful eyes had not rightly calculated the distance from the stump to the top of the pine, nor rightly weighed the power of the massed branches, and so, standing spell-bound, watching the descending trunk as one might watch his Nemesis, the rebound came and left him lying worse than dead.

Three months later, when the logs, lopped of their branches, drifted down the streams, the woodman, a human log lopped of his strength, drifted to a great city. A change, the doctor said, might prolong his life. The lumbermen made up a purse, and he started out, not very definitely knowing his destination. He had a sister, much younger than himself, who at the age of sixteen had married and gone, he believed, to Chicago. That was years ago, but he had an idea that he might find her. He was not troubled by his lack of resources: he did not believe that any man would want for a meal unless he were "shiftless." He had always been able to turn his hand to something.

He felt too ill from the jostling of the cars to notice much of anything on the journey. The dizzy scenes whirling past made him faint, and he was glad to lie with closed eyes. He imagined that his little sister in her pink calico frock and bare feet (as he remembered her) would be at the station to meet him. "Oh, Lu!" she would call from some hiding-place, and he would go and find her.

The conductor stopped by Luther's seat and said that they were in the city at last; but it seemed to the sick man as if they went miles after that, with a multitude of twinkling lights on one side and a blank darkness that they told him was the lake on the other. The conductor again stopped by his seat.

"Well, my man," said he, "how are you feeling?"

Luther, the possessor of the toughest muscles in the gang, felt a sick man's irritation at the tone of pity.

"Oh, I'm all right!" he said, gruffly, and shook off the assistance the conductor tried to offer with his overcoat. "I'm going to my sister's," he explained, in answer to the inquiry as to where he was going. The man, somewhat piqued at the spirit in which his overtures were met, left him, and Luther stepped on to the platform. There was a long *vista* of semi-light, down which crowds of people walked and baggagemen rushed. The building, if it deserved the name, seemed a ruin, and through the arched doors Luther could see men—hackmen—dancing and howling like dervishes. Trains were coming and going, and the whistles and bells kept up a ceaseless clangour. Luther, with his small satchel and uncouth dress, slouched by the crowd unnoticed, and reached the street.

He walked amid such an illumination as he had never dreamed of, and paused half blinded in the glare of a broad sheet of electric light that filled a pillared entrance into which many people passed. He looked about him. Above on every side rose great, many-windowed buildings; on the street the cars and carriages thronged, and jostling crowds dashed headlong among the vehicles. After a time he turned down a street that seemed to him a pandemonium filled with madmen. It went to his head like wine, and hardly left him the presence of mind to sustain a quiet exterior. The wind was laden with a penetrating moisture that chilled him as the dry icy breezes from Huron never had done, and the pain in his lungs made him faint and dizzy.

He wondered if his red-cheeked little sister could live in one of those vast, impregnable buildings. He thought of stopping some of those serious-looking men and asking them if they knew her, but he could not muster up the courage. The distressing experience that comes to almost every one some time in life, of losing all identity in the universal humanity, was becoming his. The tears began to roll down his wasted face from loneliness and exhaustion. He grew hungry with longing for the dirty but familiar cabins of the camp, and staggered along with eyes half closed, conjuring visions of the warm interiors, the leaping fires, the groups of laughing men seen dimly through clouds of tobacco smoke.

A delicious scent of coffee met his hungry sense and made him really think he was taking the savoury black draught from his familiar tin cup; but the muddy streets, the blinding lights, the cruel, rushing people, were still there. The buildings, however, now became different. They were lower and meaner, with dirty windows. Women laughing loudly crowded about the doors, and the establishments seemed to be equally divided between saloon-keepers, pawnbrokers, and dealers in second-hand clothes. Luther wondered where they all drew their support from. Upon one signboard he read, "Lodgings 10 cents to 50 cents. A Square Meal for 15 cents," and, thankful for some haven, entered. Here he spent his first night and other nights, while his purse dwindled and his strength waned.

At last he got a man in a drugstore to search the directory for his sister's residence. They found a name he took to be his brother-in-law's. It was two days later when he found the address—a great many-storied mansion on one of the southern boulevards—and found also that his search had been in vain. Sore and faint, he staggered back to his miserable shelter, only to arise feverish and ill in the morning. He frequented the great shop doors, thronged with brilliantly dressed ladies, and watched to see if his little sister might not dash up in one of those satin-lined coaches and take him where he would be warm and safe and would sleep undisturbed by drunken, ribald songs and loathsome surroundings. There were days when he almost forgot his name, and, striving to remember, would lose his senses for a moment and drift back to the harmonious solitudes of the North and breathe the resin-scented frosty atmosphere. He grew terrified at the blood he coughed from his lacerated lungs, and wondered bitterly why the boys did not come to take him home.

One day, as he painfully dragged himself down a residence street, he tried to collect his thoughts and form some plan for the future. He had no trade, understood no handiwork: he could fell trees! He looked at the gaunt, scrawny, transplanted specimens that met his eye, and gave himself up to the homesickness that filled his soul. He slept that night in the shelter of a stable, and spent his last money in the morning for a biscuit.

He travelled many miles that afternoon looking for something to which he might turn his hand. Once he got permission to carry a hod for half an hour. At the end of that time he fainted. When he recovered, the foreman paid him twenty-five cents. "For God's sake, man, go home," he said. Luther stared at him with a white face and went on.

There came days when he so forgot his native dignity as to beg. He seldom received anything; he was referred to various charitable institutions whose existence he had never heard of.

One morning, when a pall of smoke enveloped the city and the odours of coal-gas refused to lift their nauseating poison through the heavy air, Luther, chilled with dew and famished, awoke to a happier life. The loneliness at his heart was gone. The feeling of hopeless imprisonment that the miles and miles of streets had terrified him with gave place to one of freedom and exaltation. Above him he heard the rasping of pine boughs; his feet trod on a rebounding mat of decay; the sky was as coldly blue as the bosom of Huron. He walked as if on ether, singing a senseless jargon the woodmen had aroused the echoes with:

Hi yi halloo
The owl sees you!
Look what you do!

Hi yi halloo!

Swung over his shoulder was a stick he had used to assist his limping gait, but now transformed into the beloved axe. He would reach the clearing soon, he thought, and strode on like a giant, while people hurried from his path. Suddenly a smooth trunk, stripped of its bark and bleached by weather, arose before him.

"*Hi yi halloo!*" High went the wasted arm—crash!—a broken staff, a jingle of wires, a maddened, shouting man the centre of a group of amused spectators! 'A few moments later, four broad-shouldered men in blue had him in their grasp, pinioned and guarded, clattering over the noisy streets behind two spirited horses. They drew after them a troop of noisy, jeering boys, who danced about the wagon like a swirl of autumn leaves. Then came a halt, and Luther was dragged up the steps of a square brick building with a belfry on the top. They entered a large bare room with benches ranged about the walls, and brought him before a man at a desk.

"What is your name?" asked the man at the desk.

"*Hi yi halloo!*" said Luther.

"He's drunk, sergeant," said one of the men in blue, and the axe-man was led into the basement. He was conscious of an in-voluntary resistance, a short struggle, and a final shock of pain—then oblivion.

The chopper awoke to the realization of three stone walls and an iron grating in front. Through this he looked out upon a stone flooring across which was a row of similar apartments. He neither knew nor cared where he was. The feeling of imprison-ment was no greater than he had felt on the endless, cheerless streets. He laid himself on the bench that ran along a side wall, and, closing his eyes, listened to the babble of the clear stream and the thunder of the "drive" on its journey. How the logs hurried and jostled! crushing, whirling, ducking, with the merry lads leaping about them with shouts and laughter.

Suddenly he was recalled by a voice. Someone handed a nar-row tin cup full of coffee and a thick slice of bread through the grating. Across the way he dimly saw a man eating a similar slice of bread. Men in other compartments were swearing and singing, He knew these now for the voices he had heard in his dreams. He tried to force some of the bread down his parched and swollen throat, but failed; the coffee strangled him, and he threw himself upon the bench.

The forest again, the night-wind, the whistle of the axe through the air! Once when he opened his eyes he found it dark! It would soon be time to go to work. He fancied there would be hoarfrost on the trees in the morning. How close the cabin seemed! Ha!—here came his little sister. Her voice sounded like the wind on a spring morning. How loud it swelled now! "Lu! Lu!" she cried.

The next morning the lock-up keeper opened the cell door. Luther lay with his head in a pool of blood. His soul had escaped from the thrall of the forest.

"Well, well!" said the little fat police justice, when he was told of it. "We ought to have a doctor around to look after such cases."

A Mountain Woman

If Leroy Brainard had not had such a respect for literature, he would have written a book.

As it was, he played at being an architect—and succeeded in being a charming fellow. My sister Jessica never lost an opportunity of laughing at his endeavours as an architect.

"You can build an enchanting villa, but what would you do with a cathedral?"

"I shall never have a chance at a cathedral," he would reply. "And, besides, it always seems to me so material and so impertinent to build a little structure of stone and wood in which to worship God!"

You see what he was like? He was frivolous, yet one could never tell when he would become eloquently earnest.

Brainard went off suddenly Westward one day. I suspected that Jessica was at the bottom of it, but I asked no questions; and I did not hear from him for months. Then I got a letter from Colorado.

I have married a mountain woman. None of your puny breed of modern femininity, but a remnant left over from the heroic ages,—a primitive woman, grand and vast of spirit, capable of true and steadfast wifehood. No sophistry about her; no knowledge even that there is sophistry. Heavens! man, do you remember the *rondeaux* and *triolets* I used to write to those pretty creatures back East? It would take a Saga man of the old Norseland to write for my mountain woman. If I were an artist, I would paint her with the north star in her locks and her feet on purple cloud. I suppose you are at the Pier. I know you usually are at this season. At any rate, I shall direct this letter thither, and will follow close after it. I want my wife to see something of life. And I want her to meet your sister.

"Dear me!" cried Jessica, when I read the letter to her; "I don't know that I care to meet anything quite so gigantic as that mountain woman. I'm one of the puny breed of modern femininity, you know. I don't think my nerves can stand the encounter."

"Why, Jessica!" I protested. She blushed a little.

"Don't think bad of me, Victor. But, you see, I've a little scrap-book of those *triolets* upstairs." Then she burst into a peal of irresistible laughter. "I'm not laughing because I am piqued," she said frankly. "Though any one will admit that it is rather irritating to have a man who left you in a blasted condition re-cover with such extraordinary promptness. As a philanthropist, one of course rejoices, but as a woman, Victor, it must be admit-ted that one has a right to feel annoyed. But, honestly, I am not ungenerous, and I am going to do him a favour. I shall write, and urge him not to bring his wife here. A primitive woman, with the north star in her hair, would look well down there in the Casino eating a pineapple ice, wouldn't she? It's all very well to have a soul, you know; but it won't keep you from looking like a guy among women who have good dressmakers. I shudder at the thought of what the poor thing will suffer if he brings her here."

Jessica wrote, as she said she would; but, for all that, a fort-night later she was walking down the wharf with the "mountain woman," and I was sauntering beside Leroy. At dinner Jessica gave me no chance to talk with our friend's wife, and I only caught the quiet *contralto* tones of her voice now and then con-trasting with Jessica's vivacious *soprano*. A drizzling rain came up from the east with nightfall. Little groups of shivering men and women sat about in the parlours at the card-tables, and one blond woman sang love songs. The Brainards were tired with their journey, and left us early. When they were gone, Jessica burst into eulogy.

"That is the first woman," she declared, "I ever met who would make a fit heroine for a book."

"Then you will not feel under obligations to educate her, as you insinuated the other day?"

"Educate her! I only hope she will help me to unlearn some of the things I know. I never saw such simplicity. It is antique!"

"You're sure it's not mere vacuity?" "Victor! How can you? But you haven't talked with her. You must tomorrow. Good-night." She gathered up her trailing skirts and started down the corridor. Suddenly she turned back. "For Heaven's sake!" she whispered, in an awed tone, "I never even noticed what she had on!"

The next morning early we made up a riding party, and I rode with Mrs. Brainard. She was as tall as I, and sat in her saddle as if quite unconscious of her animal. The road stretched hard and inviting under our horses' feet. The wind smelled salt. The sky was ragged with gray masses of cloud scudding across the blue. I was beginning to glow with exhilaration, when suddenly my companion drew in her horse.

"If you do not mind, we will go back," she said.

Her tone was dejected. I thought she was tired.

"Oh, no!" she protested, when I apologized for my thoughtlessness in bringing her so far. "I'm not tired. I can ride all day. Where I come from, we have to ride if we want to go anywhere; but here there seems to be no particular place to—to reach."

"Are you so utilitarian?" I asked, laughingly. "Must you always have some reason for everything you do? I do so many things just for the mere pleasure of doing them, I'm afraid you will have a very poor opinion of me."

"That is not what I mean," she said, flushing, and turning her large gray eyes on me. "You must not think I have a reason for everything I do." She was very earnest, and it was evident that she was unacquainted with the art of making conversation. "But what I mean," she went on, "is that there is no place—no end—

to reach." She looked back over her shoulder toward the west, where the trees marked the sky line, and an expression of loss and dissatisfaction came over her face. "You see," she said, apologetically, "I'm used to different things—to the mountains. I have never been where I could not see them before in my life."

"Ah, I see! I suppose it is odd to look up and find them not there."

"It's like being lost, this not having anything around you. At least, I mean," she continued slowly, as if her thought could not easily put itself in words,—"I mean it seems as if a part of the world had been taken down. It makes you feel lonesome, as if you were living after the world had begun to die."

"You'll get used to it in a few days. It seems very beautiful to me here. And then you will have so much life to divert you."

"Life? But there is always that everywhere."

"I mean men and women."

"Oh! Still, I am not used to them. I think I might be not—not very happy with them. They might think me queer. I think I would like to show your sister the mountains."

"She has seen them often."

"Oh, she told me. But I don't mean those pretty green hills such as we saw coming here. They are not like my mountains. I like mountains that go beyond the clouds, with terrible shadows in the hollows, and belts of snow lying in the gorges where the sun cannot reach, and the snow is blue in the sunshine, or shining till you think it is silver, and the mist so wonderful all about it, changing each moment and drifting up and down, that you cannot tell what name to give the colours. These mountains of yours here in the East are so quiet; mine are shouting all the time, with the pines and the rivers. The echoes are so loud in the valley that sometimes, when the wind is rising, we can hardly hear a man talk unless he raises his voice.

"There are four cataracts near where I live, and they all have different voices, just as people do; and one of them is happy—a little white cataract—and it falls where the sun shines earliest, and till night it is shining. But the others only get the sun now

40

and then, and they are more noisy and cruel. One of them is always in the shadow, and the water looks black. That is partly because the rocks all underneath it are black. It falls down twenty great ledges in a gorge with black sides, and a white mist dances all over it at every leap. I tell father the mist is the ghost of the waters. No man ever goes there; it is too cold. The chill strikes through one, and makes your heart feel as if you were dying. But all down the side of the mountain, toward the south and the west, the sun shines on the granite and draws long points of light out of it. Father tells me soldiers marching look that way when the sun strikes on their bayonets. Those are the kind of mountains I mean, Mr. Grant."

She was looking at me with her face transfigured, as if it, like the mountains she told me of, had been lying in shadow, and waiting for the dazzling dawn.

"I had a terrible dream once," she went on; "the most terrible dream ever I had. I dreamt that the mountains had all been taken down, and that I stood on a plain to which there was no end. The sky was burning up, and the grass scorched brown from the heat, and it was twisting as if it were in pain. And animals, but no other person save myself, only wild things, were crouching and looking up at that sky. They could not run because there was no place to which to go."

"You were having a vision of the last man," I said. "I wonder myself sometimes whether this old globe of ours is going to collapse suddenly and take us with her, or whether we will disappear through slow disastrous ages of fighting and crushing, with hunger and blight to help us to the end. And then, at the last, perhaps, some luckless fellow, stronger than the rest, will stand amid the ribs of the rotting earth and go mad."

The woman's eyes were fixed on me, large and luminous. "Yes," she said; "he would go mad from the lonesomeness of it. He would be afraid to be left alone like that with God. No one would want to be taken into God's secrets."

"And our last man," I went on, "would have to stand there on that swaying wreck till even the sound of the crumbling earth

41

ceased. And he would try to find a voice and would fail, because silence would have come again. And then the light would go out—"

The shudder that crept over her made me stop, ashamed of myself.

"You talk like father," she said, with a long-drawn breath. Then she looked up suddenly at the sun shining through a rift in those reckless gray clouds, and put out one hand as if to get it full of the headlong rollicking breeze. "But the earth is not dying," she cried. "It is well and strong, and it likes to go round and round among all the other worlds. It likes the sun and moon; they are all good friends; and it likes the people who live on it. Maybe it is they instead of the fire within who keep it warm; or maybe it is warm just from always going, as we are when we run. We are young, you and I, Mr. Grant, and Leroy, and your beautiful sister, and the world is young too!" Then she laughed a strong splendid laugh, which had never had the joy taken out of it with drawing-room restrictions; and I laughed too, and felt that we had become very good companions indeed, and found myself warming to the joy of companionship as I had not since I was a boy at school.

That afternoon the four of us sat at a table in the Casino together. The Casino, as every one knows, is a place to amuse yourself. If you have a duty, a mission, or an aspiration, you do not take it there with you, it would be so obviously out of place; if poverty is ahead of you, you forget it; if you have brains, you hasten to conceal them; they would be a serious encumbrance.

There was a bubbling of conversation, a rustle and flutter such as there always is where there are many women. All the place was gay with flowers and with gowns as bright as the flowers. I remembered the apprehensions of my sister, and studied Leroy's wife to see how she fitted into this highly coloured picture. She was the only woman in the room who seemed to wear draperies. The jaunty slash and cut of fashionable attire were missing in the long brown folds of cloth that enveloped her figure. I felt certain that even from Jessica's standpoint she could not be called a guy. Picturesque she might be, past the point of convention, but she was not ridiculous.

"Judith takes all this very seriously," said Leroy, laughingly. "I suppose she would take even Paris seriously."

His wife smiled over at him. "Leroy says I am melancholy," she said, softly; "but I am always telling him that I am happy. He thinks I am melancholy because I do not laugh. I got out of the way of it by being so much alone. You only laugh to let someone else know you are pleased. When you are alone there is no use in laughing. It would be like explaining something to yourself."

"You are a philosopher, Judith. Mr. Max Mueller would like to know you."

"Is he a friend of yours, dear?"

Leroy blushed, and I saw Jessica curl her lip as she noticed the blush. She laid her hand on Mrs. Brainard's arm.

"Have you always been very much alone?" she inquired.

"I was born on the ranch, you know; and father was not fond of leaving it. Indeed, now he says he will never again go out of sight of it. But you can go a long journey without doing that; for it lies on a plateau in the valley, and it can be seen from three different mountain passes. Mother died there, and for that reason and others—father has had a strange life—he never wanted to go away. He brought a lady from Pennsylvania to teach me. She had wonderful learning, but she didn't make very much use of it.

"I thought if I had learning I would not waste it reading books. I would use it to—to live with. Father had a library, but I never cared for it. He was forever at books too. Of course," she hastened to add, noticing the look of mortification deepen on her husband's face, "I like books very well if there is nothing better at hand. But I always said to Mrs. Windsor—it was she who taught me—why read what other folk have been thinking when you can go out and think yourself? Of course one prefers one's own thoughts, just as one prefers one's own ranch, or one's own father."

"Then you are sure to like New York when you go there to

live," cried Jessica; "for there you will find something to make life entertaining all the time. No one need fall back on books there."

"I'm not sure. I'm afraid there must be such dreadful crowds of people. Of course I should try to feel that they were all like me, with just the same sort of fears, and that it was ridiculous for us to be afraid of each other, when at heart we all meant to be kind."

Jessica fairly wrung her hands. "Heavens!" she cried. "I said you would like New York. I am afraid, my dear, that it will break your heart!"

"Oh," said Mrs. Brainard, with what was meant to be a gentle jest, "no one can break my heart except Leroy. I should not care enough about anyone else, you know."

The compliment was an exquisite one. I felt the blood creep to my own brain in a sort of vicarious rapture, and I avoided looking at Leroy lest he should dislike to have me see the happiness he must feel. The simplicity of the woman seemed to invigorate me as the cool air of her mountains might if it blew to me on some bright dawn, when I had come, fevered and sick of soul, from the city.

When we were alone, Jessica said to me: "That man has too much vanity, and he thinks it is sensitiveness. He is going to imagine that his wife makes him suffer. There's no one so brutally selfish as your sensitive man. He wants everyone to live according to his ideas, or he immediately begins suffering. That friend of yours hasn't the courage of his convictions. He is going to be ashamed of the very qualities that made him love his wife."

There was a hop that night at the hotel, quite an unusual affair as to elegance, given in honour of a woman from New York, who wrote a novel a month.

Mrs. Brainard looked so happy that night when she came in the parlour, after the music had begun, that I felt a moisture gather in my eyes just because of the beauty of her joy, and the forced vivacity of the women about me seemed suddenly coarse and insincere. Some wonderful red stones, brilliant as rubies, glittered in among the diaphanous black driftings of her dress. She asked me if the stones were not very pretty, and said she gathered them in one of her mountain river-beds.

"But the gown?" I said. "Surely, you do not gather gowns like that in river-beds, or pick them off mountain-pines?"

"But you can get them in Denver. Father always sent to Denver for my finery. He was very particular about how I looked. You see, I was all he had—" She broke off, her voice faltering.

"Come over by the window," I said, to change her thought. "I have something to repeat to you. It is a song of Sydney Lanier's. I think he was the greatest poet that ever lived in America, though not many agree with me. But he is my dear friend anyway, though he is dead, and I never saw him; and I want you to hear some of his words."

I led her across to an open window. The dancers were whirling by us. The waltz was one of those melancholy ones which speak the spirit of the dance more eloquently than any merry melody can. The sound of the sea booming beyond in the darkness came to us, and long paths of light, now red, now green, stretched toward the distant lighthouse. These were the lines I repeated:—

What heartache—ne'er a hill!
Inexorable, vapid, vague, and chill
The drear sand levels drain my spirit low.
With one poor word they tell me all they know;
Whereat their stupid tongues, to tease my pain,
Do drawl it o'er and o'er again.
They hurt my heart with griefs I cannot name;
Always the same—the same.

But I got no further. I felt myself moved with a sort of passion which did not seem to come from within, but to be communicated to me from her. A certain unfamiliar happiness pricked through with pain thrilled me, and I heard her whispering,—

"Do not go on, do not go on! I cannot stand it tonight!"

"Hush," I whispered back; "come out for a moment!" We

stole into the dusk without, and stood there trembling. I swayed with her emotion. There was a long silence. Then she said: "Father may be walking alone now by the black cataract. That is where he goes when he is sad. I can see how lonely he looks among those little twisted pines that grow from the rock. And he will be remembering all the evenings we walked there together, and all the things we said." I did not answer. Her eyes were still on the sea.

"What was the name of the man who wrote that verse you just said to me?"

I told her.

"And he is dead? Did they bury him in the mountains? No? I wish I could have put him where he could have heard those four voices calling down the canyon."

"Come back in the house," I said; "you must come, indeed," I said, as she shrank from re-entering.

Jessica was dancing like a fairy with Leroy. They both saw us and smiled as we came in, and a moment later they joined us. I made my excuses and left my friends to Jessica's care. She was a sort of social tyrant wherever she was, and I knew one word from her would insure the popularity of our friends—not that they needed the intervention of any one. Leroy had been a sort of drawing-room pet since before he stopped wearing knickerbockers.

"He is at his best in a drawing-room," said Jessica, "because there he deals with theory and not with action. And he has such beautiful theories that the women, who are all idealists, adore him."

The next morning I awoke with a conviction that I had been idling too long. I went back to the city and brushed the dust from my desk. Then each morning, I, as Jessica put it, "formed public opinion" to the extent of one column a day in the columns of a certain enterprising morning journal.

Brainard said I had treated him shabbily to leave upon the heels of his coming. But a man who works for his bread and butter must put a limit to his holiday. It is different when you only work to add to your general picturesqueness. That is what I wrote Leroy, and it was the unkindest thing I ever said to him; and why I did it I do not know to this day. I was glad, though, when he failed to answer the letter. It gave me a more reasonable excuse for feeling out of patience with him.

The days that followed were very dull. It was hard to get back into the way of working. I was glad when Jessica came home to set up our little establishment and to join in the autumn gayeties. Brainard brought his wife to the city soon after, and went to housekeeping in an odd sort of a way.

"I couldn't see anything in the place save curios," Jessica reported, after her first call on them. "I suppose there is a cooking-stove somewhere, and maybe even a pantry with pots in it. But all I saw was Alaska totems and Navajo blankets. They have as many skins around on the floor and couches as would have satisfied an ancient Briton. And everybody was calling there. You know Mr. Brainard runs to curios in selecting his friends as well as his furniture. The parlours were full this afternoon of abnormal people, that is to say, with folks one reads about. I was the only one there who hadn't done something. I guess it's because I am too healthy."

"How did Mrs. Brainard like such a motley crew?"

"She was wonderful—perfectly wonderful! Those insulting creatures were all studying her, and she knew it. But her dignity was perfect, and she looked as proud as a Sioux chief. She listened to every one, and they all thought her so bright."

"Brainard must have been tremendously proud of her."

"Oh, he was—of her and his Chilcat *portieres.*"

Jessica was there often, but—well, I was busy. At length, however, I was forced to go. Jessica refused to make any further excuses for me. The rooms were filled with small celebrities.

"We are the only nonentities," whispered Jessica, as she looked around; "it will make us quite distinguished."

We went to speak to our hostess. She stood beside her husband, looking taller than ever; and her face was white. Her long red gown of clinging silk was so peculiar as to give one the impression that she was dressed in character. It was easy to tell that it was one of Leroy's fancies. I hardly heard what she said, but I know she reproached me gently for not having been to see them. I had no further word with her till someone led her to the piano, and she paused to say,—

"That poet you spoke of to me—the one you said was a friend of yours—he is my friend now too, and I have learned to sing some of his songs. I am going to sing one now." She seemed to have no timidity at all, but stood quietly, with a half smile, while a young man with a Russian name played a strange minor prelude. Then she sang, her voice a wonderful *contralto*, cold at times, and again lit up with gleams of passion. The music itself was fitful, now full of joy, now tender, and now sad:

Look off, dear love, across the sallow sands,
And mark yon meeting of the sun and sea,
How long they kiss in sight of all the lands,
Ah! longer, longer we.

"She has a genius for feeling, hasn't she?" Leroy whispered to me.

"A genius for feeling!" I repeated, angrily. "Man, she has a heart and a soul and a brain, if that is what you mean! I shouldn't think you would be able to look at her from the standpoint of a critic."

Leroy shrugged his shoulders and went off. For a moment I almost hated him for not feeling more resentful. I felt as if he owed it to his wife to take offence at my foolish speech.

It was evident that the "mountain woman" had become the fashion. I read reports in the papers about her unique receptions. I saw her name printed conspicuously among the list of those who attended all sorts of dinners and musicales and evenings among the set that affected intellectual pursuits. She joined a number of women's clubs of an exclusive kind.

"She is doing whatever her husband tells her to," said Jessica. "Why, the other day I heard her ruining her voice on 'Siegfried'!"

But from day to day I noticed a difference in her. She developed a terrible activity. She took personal charge of the affairs of her house; she united with Leroy in keeping the house filled with guests; she got on the board of a hospital for little children, and spent a part of every day among the cots where the sufferers lay. Now and then when we spent a quiet evening alone with her and Leroy, she sewed continually on little white nightgowns for these poor babies. She used her carriage to take the most extraordinary persons riding.

"In the cause of health," Leroy used to say, "I ought to have the carriage fumigated after every ride Judith takes, for she is always accompanied by someone who looks as if he or she should go into quarantine."

One night, when he was chaffing her in this way, she flung her sewing suddenly from her and sprang to her feet, as if she were going to give way to a burst of girlish temper. Instead of that, a stream of tears poured from her eyes, and she held out her trembling hands toward Jessica.

"He does not know," she sobbed. "He cannot understand."

One memorable day Leroy hastened over to us while we were still at breakfast to say that Judith was ill,—strangely ill. All night long she had been muttering to herself as if in a delirium. Yet she answered lucidly all questions that were put to her.

"She begs for Miss Grant. She says over and over that she 'knows,' whatever that may mean."

When Jessica came home she told me she did not know. She only felt that a tumult of impatience was stirring in her friend.

"There is something majestic about her,—something epic. I feel as if she were making me live a part in some great drama, the end of which I cannot tell. She is suffering, but I cannot tell why she suffers."

Weeks went on without an abatement in this strange illness. She did not keep her bed. Indeed, she neglected few of her usual occupations. But her hands were burning, and her eyes grew bright with that wild sort of lustre one sees in the eyes of those who give themselves up to strange drugs or manias. She grew whimsical, and formed capricious friendships, only to drop them.

And then one day she closed her house to all acquaintances, and sat alone continually in her room, with her hands clasped in her lap, and her eyes swimming with the emotions that never found their way to her tongue.

Brainard came to the office to talk with me about her one day. "I am a very miserable man, Grant," he said. "I am afraid I have lost my wife's regard. Oh, don't tell me it is partly my fault. I know it well enough. And I know you haven't had a very good opinion of me lately. But I am remorseful enough now, God knows. And I would give my life to see her as she was when I found her first among the mountains. Why, she used to climb them like a strong man, and she was forever shouting and singing. And she had peopled every spot with strange modern mythological creatures.

"Her father is an old dreamer, and she got the trick from him. They had a little telescope on a great knoll in the centre of the valley, just where it commanded a long path of stars, and they used to spend nights out there when the frost literally fell in flakes. When I think how hardy and gay she was, how full of courage and life, and look at her now, so feverish and broken, I feel as if I should go mad. You know I never meant to do her any harm. Tell me that much, Grant."

"I think you were very egotistical for a while, Brainard, and that is a fact. And you didn't appreciate how much her nature demanded. But I do not think you are responsible for your wife's present condition. If there is any comfort in that statement, you are welcome to it."

"But you don't mean—" he got no further.

"I mean that your wife may have her reservations, just as we all have, and I am paying her high praise when I say it. You are not so narrow, Leroy, as to suppose for a moment that the only sort of passion a woman is capable of is that which she entertains for a man. How do I know what is going on in your wife's soul? But it is nothing which even an idealist of women, such as I am, old fellow, need regret."

How glad I was afterward that I spoke those words. They exercised a little restraint, perhaps, on Leroy when the day of his terrible trial came. They made him wrestle with the demon of suspicion that strove to possess him. I was sitting in my office, lagging dispiritedly over my work one day, when the door burst open and Brainard stood beside me. Brainard, I say, and yet in no sense the man I had known,—not a hint in this pale creature, whose breath struggled through chattering teeth, and whose hands worked in uncontrollable spasms, of the nonchalant elegant I had known. Not a glimpse to be seen in those angry and determined eyes of the gayly selfish spirit of my holiday friend.

"She's gone!" he gasped. "Since yesterday. And I'm here to ask you what you think now? And what you know."

A panorama of all shameful possibilities for one black moment floated before me. I remember this gave place to a wave, cold as death, that swept from head to foot; then Brainard's hands fell heavily on my shoulders.

"Thank God at least for this much," he said, hoarsely; "I didn't know at first but I had lost both friend and wife. But I see you know nothing. And indeed in my heart I knew all the time that you did not. Yet I had to come to you with my anger. And I remembered how you defended her. What explanation can you offer now?"

I got him to sit down after a while and tell me what little there was to tell. He had been away for a day's shooting, and when he returned he found only the perplexed servants at home. A note was left for him. He showed it to me.

There are times when we must do as we must, not as we would. I am going to do something I have been driven to do since I left my home. I do not leave any message of love for you, because you would not care for it from a woman so weak as I. But it is so easy for you to be happy that I hope in a little while you will forget the wife who yielded to an influence past resisting. It may be madness, but I am not great enough to give it up. I tried to make

51

the sacrifice, but I could not. I tried to be as gay as you, and to live your sort of life; but I could not do it. Do not make the effort to forgive me. You will be happier if you simply hold me in the contempt I deserve.

I read the letter over and over. I do not know that I believe that the spirit of inanimate things can permeate to the intelligence of man. I am sure I always laughed at such ideas. Yet holding that note with its shameful seeming words, I felt a consciousness that it was written in purity and love. And then before my eyes there came a scene so vivid that for a moment the office with its familiar furniture was obliterated. What I saw was a long firm road, green with midsummer luxuriance. The leisurely thudding of my horse's feet sounded in my ears. Beside me was a tall, black-robed figure. I saw her look back with that expression of deprivation at the sky line. "It's like living after the world has begun to die," said the pensive minor voice. "It seems as if part of the world had been taken down."

"Brainard," I yelled, "come here! I have it. Here's your explanation. I can show you a new meaning for every line of this letter. Man, she has gone to the mountains. She has gone to worship her own gods!"

Two weeks later I got a letter from Brainard, dated from Colorado.

Old man, you're right. She is here. I found my mountain woman here where the four voices of her cataracts had been calling to her. I saw her the moment our mules rounded the road that commands the valley. We had been riding all night and were drenched with cold dew, hungry to desperation, and my spirits were of lead. Suddenly we got out from behind the granite wall, and there she was, standing, where I had seen her so often, beside the little waterfall that she calls the happy one. She was looking straight up at the billowing mist that dipped down the mountain, mammoth saffron rolls of it, plunging so madly from the impetus of the wind that one marvelled how it could be noiseless.

Ah, you do not know Judith! That strange, unsophisticated, sometimes awkward woman you saw bore no more resemblance to my mountain woman than I to Hercules. How strong and beautiful she looked standing there wrapped in an ecstasy! It was my primitive woman back in her primeval world. How the blood leaped in me! All my old romance, so different from the common love-histories of most men, was there again within my reach! All the mystery, the poignant happiness were mine again. Do not hold me in contempt because I show you my heart. You saw my misery. Why should I grudge you a glimpse of my happiness? She saw me when I touched her hand, not before, so wrapped was she. But she did not seem surprised. Only in her splendid eyes there came a large content. She pointed to the dancing little white fall. 'I thought something wonderful was going to happen,' she whispered, 'for it has been laughing so.'

I shall not return to New York. I am going to stay here with my mountain woman, and I think perhaps I shall find out what life means here sooner than I would back there with you. I shall learn to see large things large and small things small. Judith says to tell you and Miss Grant that the four voices are calling for you every day in the valley.

Yours in fullest friendship,

Leroy Brainard.

An Astral Onion

When Tig Braddock came to Nora Finnegan he was red-headed and freckled, and, truth to tell, he remained with these features to the end of his life—a life prolonged by a lucky, if somewhat improbable, incident, as you shall hear.

Tig had shuffled off his parents as saurians, of some sorts, do their skins. During the temporary absence from home of his mother, who was at the bridewell, and the more extended vacation of his father, who, like Villon, loved the open road and the life of it, Tig, who was not a well-domesticated animal, wandered away. The humane society never heard of him, the neighbours did not miss him, and the law took no cognizance of this detached citizen—this lost pleiad. Tig would have sunk into that melancholy which is attendant upon hunger,—the only form of despair which babyhood knows,—if he had not wandered across the path of Nora Finnegan. Now Nora shone with steady brightness in her orbit, and no sooner had Tig entered her atmosphere, than he was warmed and comforted. Hunger could not live where Nora was. The basement room where she kept house was redolent with savoury smells; and in the stove in her front room—which was also her bedroom—there was a bright fire glowing when fire was needed.

Nora went out washing for a living. But she was not a poor washerwoman. Not at all. She was a washerwoman triumphant. She had perfect health, an enormous frame, an abounding enthusiasm for life, and a rich abundance of professional pride. She believed herself to be the best washer of white clothes she had ever had the pleasure of knowing, and the value placed upon her services, and her long connection with certain families with large weekly washings, bore out this estimate of herself—an estimate which she never endeavoured to conceal.

Nora had buried two husbands without being unduly depressed by the fact. The first husband had been a disappointment, and Nora winked at Providence when an accident in a tunnel carried him off—that is to say, carried the husband off. The second husband was not so much of a disappointment as a surprise. He developed ability of a literary order, and wrote songs which sold and made him a small fortune. Then he ran away with another woman. The woman spent his fortune, drove him to dissipation, and when he was dying he came back to Nora, who received him cordially, attended him to the end, and cheered his last hours by singing his own songs to him. Then she raised a headstone recounting his virtues, which were quite numerous, and refraining from any reference to those peculiarities which had caused him to be such a surprise.

Only one actual chagrin had ever nibbled at the sound heart of Nora Finnegan—a cruel chagrin, with long, white teeth, such as rodents have! She had never held a child to her breast, nor laughed in its eyes; never bathed the pink form of a little son or daughter; never felt a tugging of tiny hands at her voluminous calico skirts! Nora had burnt many candles before the statue of the blessed Virgin without remedying this deplorable condition. She had sent up unavailing prayers—she had, at times, wept hot tears of longing and loneliness. Sometimes in her sleep she dreamed that a wee form, warm and exquisitely soft, was pressed against her firm body, and that a hand with tiniest pink nails crept within her bosom. But as she reached out to snatch this delicious little creature closer, she woke to realize a barren woman's grief, and turned herself in anguish on her lonely pillow.

So when Tig came along, accompanied by two curs, who had faithfully followed him from his home, and when she learned the details of his story, she took him in, curs and all, and, having bathed the three of them, made them part and parcel of her home. This was after the demise of the second husband, and at a time when Nora felt that she had done all a woman could be expected to do for Hymen.

Tig was a preposterous baby. The curs were preposterous curs. Nora had always been afflicted with a surplus amount of laughter—laughter which had difficulty in attaching itself to anything, owing to the lack of the really comic in the surroundings of the poor. But with a red-headed and freckled baby boy and two trick dogs in the house, she found a good and sufficient excuse for her hilarity, and would have torn the cave where echo lies with her mirth, had that cave not been at such an immeasurable distance from the crowded neighbourhood where she lived.

At the age of four Tig went to free kindergarten; at the age of six he was in school, and made three grades the first year and two the next. At fifteen he was graduated from the high school and went to work as errand boy in a newspaper office, with the fixed determination to make a journalist of himself.

Nora was a trifle worried about his morals when she discovered his intellect, but as time went on, and Tig showed no devotion for any woman save herself, and no consciousness that there were such things as bad boys or saloons in the world, she began to have confidence. All of his earnings were brought to her. Every holiday was spent with her. He told her his secrets and his aspirations. He admitted that he expected to become a great man, and, though he had not quite decided upon the nature of his career,—saving, of course, the makeshift of journalism,—it was not unlikely that he would elect to be a novelist like—well, probably like Thackeray.

Hope, always a charming creature, put on her most alluring smiles for Tig, and he made her his mistress, and feasted on the light of her eyes. Moreover, he was chaperoned, so to speak, by Nora Finnegan, who listened to every line Tig wrote, and made a mighty applause, and filled him up with good Irish stew, many coloured as the coat of Joseph, and pungent with the inimitable perfume of "the rose of the cellar." Nora Finnegan understood the onion, and used it lovingly. She perceived the difference between the use and abuse of this pleasant and obvious friend of hungry man, and employed it with enthusiasm, but discretion. Thus it came about that whoever ate of her dinners, found the meals of other cooks strangely lacking in savour, and remembered with regret the soups and stews, the broiled steaks, and stuffed chickens of the woman who appreciated the onion.

When Nora Finnegan came home with a cold one day, she took it in such a jocular fashion that Tig felt not the least concern about her, and when, two days later, she died of pneumonia, he almost thought, at first, that it must be one of her jokes. She had departed with decision, such as had characterized every act of her life, and had made as little trouble for others as possible. When she was dead the community had the opportunity of discovering the number of her friends. Miserable children with faces which revealed two generations of hunger, homeless boys with vicious countenances, miserable wrecks of humanity, women with bloated faces, came to weep over Nora's bier, and to lay a flower there, and to scuttle away, more abjectly lonely than even sin could make them.

If the cats and the dogs, the sparrows and horses to which she had shown kindness, could also have attended her funeral, the procession would have been, from a point of numbers, one of the most imposing the city had ever known. Tig used up all their savings to bury her, and the next week, by some peculiar fatality, he had a falling out with the night editor of his paper, and was discharged. This sank deep into his sensitive soul, and he swore he would be an underling no longer—which foolish resolution was directly traceable to his hair, the colour of which, it will be recollected, was red.

Not being an underling, he was obliged to make himself into something else, and he recurred passionately to his old idea of becoming a novelist. He settled down in Nora's basement rooms, went to work on a battered type-writer, did his own cooking, and occasionally pawned something to keep him in food. The environment was calculated to further impress him with the idea of his genius.

A certain magazine offered an alluring prize for a short story, and Tig wrote one, and rewrote it, making alterations, revisions, annotations, and interlineations which would have reflected credit upon Honoré; Balzac himself. Then he wrought all together, with splendid brevity and dramatic force,—Tig's own words,—and mailed the same. He was convinced he would get the prize. He was just as much convinced of it as Nora Finnegan would have been if she had been with him.

So he went about doing more fiction, taking no especial care of himself, and wrapt in rosy dreams, which, not being warm enough for the weather, permitted him to come down with rheumatic fever.

He lay alone in his room and suffered such torments as the condemned and rheumatic know, depending on one of Nora's former friends to come in twice a day and keep up the fire for him. This friend was aged ten, and looked like a sparrow who had been in a cyclone, but somewhere inside his bones was a wit which had spelled out devotion. He found fuel for the cracked stove, somehow or other. He brought it in a dirty sack which he carried on his back, and he kept warmth in Tig's miserable body. Moreover, he found food of a sort—cold, horrible bits often, and Tig wept when he saw them, remembering the meals Nora had served him.

Tig was getting better, though he was conscious of a weak heart and a lamenting stomach, when, to his amazement, the sparrow ceased to visit him. Not for a moment did Tig suspect desertion. He knew that only something in the nature of an act of Providence, as the insurance companies would designate it, could keep the little bundle of bones away from him. As the days went by, he became convinced of it, for no sparrow came, and no coal lay upon the hearth. The basement window fortunately looked toward the south, and the pale April sunshine was beginning to make itself felt, so that the temperature of the room was not unbearable. But Tig languished; sank, sank, day by day, and was kept alive only by the conviction that the letter announcing the award of the thousand-dollar prize would presently come to him.

One night he reached a place, where, for hunger and dejection, his mind wandered, and he seemed to be complaining all night to Nora of his woes. When the chill dawn came, with chittering of little birds on the dirty pavement, and an agitation of the scrawny willow "pussies," he was not able to lift his hand to his head. The window before his sight was but "a glimmering square." He said to himself that the end must be at hand. Yet it was cruel, cruel, with fame and fortune so near! If only he had some food, he might summon strength to rally—just for a little while! Impossible that he should die! And yet without food there was no choice.

Dreaming so of Nora's dinners, thinking how one spoonful of a stew such as she often compounded would now be his salvation, he became conscious of the presence of a strong perfume in the room. It was so familiar that it seemed like a sub-consciousness, yet he found no name for this friendly odour for a bewildered minute or two. Little by little, however, it grew upon him, that it was the onion—that fragrant and kindly bulb which had attained its apotheosis in the cuisine of Nora Finnegan of sacred memory. He opened his languid eyes, to see if, mayhap, the plant had not attained some more palpable materialization.

Behold, it was so! Before him, in a brown earthen dish,—a most familiar dish,—was an onion, pearly white, in placid seas of gravy, smoking and delectable. With unexpected strength he raised himself, and reached for the dish, which floated before him in a halo made by its own steam. It moved toward him, offered a spoon to his hand, and as he ate he heard about the room the rustle of Nora Finnegan's starched skirts, and now and then a faint, faint echo of her old-time laugh—such an echo as one may find of the sea in the heart of a shell.

The noble bulb disappeared little by little before his voracity, and in contentment greater than virtue can give, he sank back upon his pillow and slept.

Two hours later the postman knocked at the door, and receiving no answer, forced his way in. Tig, half awake, saw him enter with no surprise. He felt no surprise when he put a letter in his hand bearing the name of the magazine to which he had sent his short story. He was not even surprised, when, tearing it open with suddenly alert hands, he found within the check for the first prize—the check he had expected.

All that day, as the April sunlight spread itself upon his floor, he felt his strength grow. Late in the afternoon the sparrow came back, paler, and more bony than ever, and sank, breathing hard, upon the floor, with his sack of coal.

"I've been sick," he said, trying to smile. "Terrible sick, but I come as soon as I could."

"Build up the fire," cried Tig, in a voice so strong it made the sparrow start as if a stone had struck him. "Build up the fire, and forget you are sick. For, by the shade of Nora Finnegan, you shall be hungry no more!"

A Spectral Collie

William Percy Cecil happened to be a younger son, so he left home—which was England—and went to Kansas to ranch it. Thousands of younger sons do the same, only their destination is not invariably Kansas.

An agent at Wichita picked out Cecil's farm for him and sent the deeds over to England before Cecil left. He said there was a house on the place. So Cecil's mother fitted him out for America just as she had fitted out another superfluous boy for Africa, and parted from him with an heroic front and big agonies of mother-ache which she kept to herself.

The boy bore up the way a man of his blood ought, but when he went out to the kennel to see Nita, his collie, he went to pieces somehow, and rolled on the grass with her in his arms and wept like a booby. But the remarkable part of it was that Nita wept too, big, hot dog tears which her master wiped away. When he went off she howled like a hungry baby, and had to be switched before she would give anyone a night's sleep.

When Cecil got over on his Kansas place he fitted up the shack as cosily as he could, and learned how to fry bacon and make soda biscuits. Incidentally, he did farming, and sunk a heap of money, finding out how not to do things. Meantime, the Americans laughed at him, and were inclined to turn the cold shoulder, and his compatriots, of whom there were a number in the county, did not prove to his liking. They consoled themselves for their exiled state in fashions not in keeping with Cecil's traditions. His homesickness went deeper than theirs, perhaps, and

American whiskey could not make up for the loss of his English home, nor flirtations with the gay American village girls quite compensate him for the loss of his English mother. So he kept to himself and had nostalgia as some men have consumption.

At length the loneliness got so bad that he had to see some living thing from home, or make a flunk of it and go back like a cry baby. He had a stiff pride still, though he sobbed himself to sleep more than one night, as many a pioneer has done before him. So he wrote home for Nita, the collie, and got word that she would be sent. Arrangements were made for her care all along the line, and she was properly boxed and shipped.

As the time drew near for her arrival, Cecil could hardly eat. He was too excited to apply himself to anything. The day of her expected arrival he actually got up at five o'clock to clean the house and make it look as fine as possible for her inspection. Then he hitched up and drove fifteen miles to get her. The train pulled out just before he reached the station, so Nita in her box was waiting for him on the platform. He could see her in a queer way, as one sees the purple centre of a revolving circle of light; for, to tell the truth, with the long ride in the morning sun, and the beating of his heart, Cecil was only about half-conscious of anything. He wanted to yell, but he didn't. He kept himself in hand and lifted up the sliding side of the box and called to Nita, and she came out.

But it wasn't the man who fainted, though he might have done so, being crazy homesick as he was, and half-fed and over-worked while he was yet soft from an easy life. No, it was the dog! She looked at her master's face, gave one cry of inexpressible joy, and fell over in a real feminine sort of a faint, and had to be brought to like any other lady, with camphor and water and a few drops of spirit down her throat. Then Cecil got up on the wagon seat, and she sat beside him with her head on his arm, and they rode home in absolute silence, each feeling too much for speech. After they reached home, however, Cecil showed her all over the place, and she barked out her ideas in glad sociability.

After that Cecil and Nita were inseparable. She walked beside him all day when he was out with the cultivator, or when he was mowing or reaping. She ate beside him at table and slept across his feet at night. Evenings when he looked over the *Graphic* from home, or read the books his mother sent him, that he might keep in touch with the world, Nita was beside him, patient, but jealous. Then, when he threw his book or paper down and took her on his knee and looked into her pretty eyes, or frolicked with her, she fairly laughed with delight.

In short, she was faithful with that faith of which only a dog is capable—that unquestioning faith to which even the most loving women never quite attain.

However, Fate was annoyed at this perfect friendship. It didn't give her enough to do, and Fate is a restless thing with a horrible appetite for variety. So poor Nita died one day mysteriously, and gave her last look to Cecil as a matter of course; and he held her paws till the last moment, as a stanch friend should, and laid her away decently in a pine box in the cornfield, where he could be shielded from public view if he chose to go there now and then and sit beside her grave.

He went to bed very lonely, indeed, the first night. The shack seemed to him to be removed endless miles from the other habitations of men. He seemed cut off from the world, and ached to hear the cheerful little barks which Nita had been in the habit of giving him by way of goodnight. Her amiable eye with its friendly light was missing, the gay wag of her tail was gone; all her ridiculous ways, at which he was never tired of laughing, were things of the past.

He lay down, busy with these thoughts, yet so habituated to Nita's presence, that when her weight rested upon his feet, as usual, he felt no surprise. But after a moment it came to him that as she was dead the weight he felt upon his feet could not be hers. And yet, there it was, warm and comfortable, cuddling down in the familiar way. He actually sat up and put his hand down to the foot of the bed to discover what was there. But there was nothing there, save the weight. And that stayed with him that night and many nights after.

It happened that Cecil was a fool, as men will be when they are young, and he worked too hard, and didn't take proper care of himself; and so it came about that he fell sick with a low fever. He struggled around for a few days, trying to work it off, but one morning he awoke only to the consciousness of absurd dreams. He seemed to be on the sea, sailing for home, and the boat was tossing and pitching in a weary circle, and could make no headway. His heart was burning with impatience, but the boat went round and round in that endless circle till he shrieked out with agony.

The next neighbours were the Taylors, who lived two miles and a half away. They were awakened that morning by the howling of a dog before their door. It was a hideous sound and would give them no peace. So Charlie Taylor got up and opened the door, discovering there an excited little collie.

"Why, Tom," he called, "I thought Cecil's collie was dead!"

"She is," called back Tom.

"No, she ain't neither, for here she is, shakin' like an aspin, and a beggin' me to go with her. Come out, Tom, and see."

It was Nita, no denying, and the men, perplexed, followed her to Cecil's shack, where they found him babbling.

But that was the last of her. Cecil said he never felt her on his feet again. She had performed her final service for him, he said. The neighbours tried to laugh at the story at first, but they knew the Taylors wouldn't take the trouble to lie, and as for Cecil, no one would have ventured to chaff him.

"Covers for Twelve"

He was glad she was beautiful. He liked to take a beautiful woman in to dinner. He noticed the diamond star in her hair, and he noticed, too, the pink tint of her bare shoulders, and the curves, full and tender, sweeping down from her chin. Her eyes were dark and narrow and sidelong in their glance, and suited the perfume of sandalwood that came from her gown. They did not speak as they walked down the long hall together between the palms. But when they were at the table and he had looked casually up and down the length of it, he said to her:

"This is a very beautiful scene."

She looked up and down the glittering length, too, and then at him with those oriental eyes.

"Is it?" she said.

"Why do you question it?" he asked.

"Why?" she repeated, "because I see not only the substance of things that are, but also the shadow of things not seen."

It was those words, or the odour of the sandalwood, or the mystery of her glance, or something that he could not name, that seemed to bring the whole pleasant pageant of the feast before him, not as if he were a part of it, but as if it were a scene that he was watching from afar. The lilies nodded among the ferns down the length of the table, and the crystal dishes caught the rosy gleam of the light in a thousand facets. The glasses stood grouped before each plate, like fragments of the prism, purple, red, and yellow, in blendings fair as an opal. The servants moved noiselessly about the lofty room, studiedly obsequious.

The voices of the women, gay and excited, broke on the ear sharply. Why must they all be gay, he wondered. Why should they all laugh so? One wore pearls about her neck; one had English violets; one showed the deep wrinkles of pride in her face; one was timid, and bore her shameless gown with a sort of innocent protest, yielding up her maiden modesty to satisfy a fashion. One was splendid, with large, sophisticated eyes. She knew the world, and the ways of it. Her hair was the colour, of corn and her dress was like the poppy.

As for the men, they seemed very tired. They laughed, too, and were pleased with the women, and the number of glasses before their plates, and the flavour of the soup. But still their faces showed a weariness, as if life drove them hard.

Over this vision—for vision it all seemed—began to float other visions, as the painted screens fall one over the other in a transformation scene. The first one that fell was gray, yet through it and beyond it glowed those mellow lights, and glittered the crystal, and the yellow wine in the glasses sent up scintillations, as shallows do in the sunshine. The gray scene was foremost, though, and showed the interior of a room. Someone—was it the soul of the woman beside him, with the mystery in her eyes—seemed to lead along a wind-swept street to this room, he seeing it all the time and knowing it for their destination. The paper had peeled from the walls; rags of curtains hung at the windows; there was a dim light from a smoking lamp, but no other glow there, neither of fire nor hope nor illumination.

Once within the room, she who led him pointed to the bed where two children lay shuddering under ragged coverings. In a ruin of a cart near by the bed a baby lay, holding in its puny hands the form of a frowsy doll. A woman, with chattering teeth and a shivering form, huddled by the cart, jogging it slightly with her hand. In her face was a look of fear and suffering, such as an animal might wear.

Up and down the floor, and ever up and down, there paced a man. He alone seemed not to feel the cold. His cheeks were hectic. He was worn with disease, yet now his mental torture galvanized him. Sometimes he paused by the bed where the children huddled together under their thin coverlet. Sometimes he stopped beside the broken cart and looked at the white face of his little one. A moan broke through his wife's clenched teeth.

"We are dying!" she said; "we are dying!"

The flush in the man's face became deeper. An angry flush—angry almost to madness—leaped in his eyes; he looked for a moment as if he might have put a knife in her heart. But instead he put on his hat and rushed from the house. Just without a network of iron roads made their way past the building. On a siding stood three cars full to the top with coal—coal, which is warmth and life and happiness! There was an old basket there, and the man filled it, very cautiously, so that the dark, shining particles would not make a noise as they fell together. But as the basket was filled a hand dropped on his shoulder.

The two men eyed each other a moment.

"You're caught," said one.

"G—d d—n you!"

"Come on. I'm here to watch for the likes of you."

"D—n you!"

"Come on."

The other put his hands to his mouth and shouted:

"Molly! Molly!"

The upper window of that wretched room opened, and the woman put her head out. The gust blew out the smoking flame of the lamp.

"If you're not dead by morning, you might look for me down in the city jail!"

"No coal?" asked the other man, watching the head of the woman. The man he spoke to looked silently at him, as if he were his murderer. The two walked on together down the track. The woman drew within the room and closed the window. Then she threw herself upon the floor. The baby waked and wailed. The woman ground her teeth but did not move.

The gray scene seemed to sink out of sight. Another came, in darker colours yet. It was a neat room, with touches of taste in it.

The room was vacant—with a terrible vacancy, as if something had gone, never to return. The chairs had a formidable orderliness about them, sitting as they did, backed close against the wall. Out in the centre of the room were two standards, such as coffins rest on. In the windows came trooping the shadows of the winter twilight, and in at the door came other forms, not shadows, though they walked in the shadow. The man stopped before the spot where the coffin had been. The children stood there too. They remembered that their mother would never again light the lamp nor spread the table for supper. No savoury smell greeted them. The shadows thronged in over the window-sill—shadows of hunger, loneliness, cold, misery and sin. The father saw them. He looked at the children—for whom there was no mother's kiss. He looked at his hands—for which there was no work.

"Who killed her?" he cried in hoarse anger. "It was not I. Yet she is dead. She has been murdered!"

The children fled from him, sobbing, into the room beyond. Still the shadows trooped in and thronged around the man.

This scene sank too, and another took its place.

It was in the store where the county doles out its food to the hungry and its fuel to the cold. The room was large, yet it was full. Women with sad eyes, men with desperate faces, little children ragged and pinched, crowded there together, waiting with terrible patience for their turn—for their chance of a little more life.

"It's a bad scene," said one of the men who was handing out the food, to another one. "Bad?" said the other. "It's not so bad as a scene we may see here soon."

The first man did not ask what that scene might be. He only said, as he handed over a package to a woman with a face half mad with want, "Am I my brother's keeper?"

And suddenly the scene changed in a twinkling, and all of gold and whiteness was the vision before him.

A wondrous place filled with sunshine to the eye and ecstasy to the spirit. And he who saw these things knew it was heaven, because happiness and satisfaction were there, and he heard from voices stern and beautiful a chorus louder than the voice of the sea when the equinox is upon it.

"Thou art thy brother's keeper. Beware of the trust betrayed!"

Then all the wonder and the harmony ceased. He was back again at the dinner table, and the din was in his ears, the odour of rare wine in his senses, and the woman beside him was brooding, with her mystical gaze. He felt in thrall to her, as if she were the one who owned his body and his soul; and he said:

"Do you know what I have seen since I sat here?"

"A vision," she said, "is as a lightning's flash. See! while you dreamed the dish before you has not cooled. Shadows need no space, not even in time. And now the shadows of things not seen have come and gone. Yours is the substance of things that are. Then eat and be merry, for tomorrow you die."

"I am my brother's keeper," said he, "and I shall never be merry again. For the times are upon us, and the rumblings of the storm are here."

From the Loom of the Dead

When Urda Bjarnason tells a tale all the men stop their talking to listen, for they know her to be wise with the wisdom of the old people, and that she has more learning than can be got even from the great schools at Reykjavik. She is especially prized by them here in this new country where the Icelandmen are settled—this America, so new in letters, where the people speak foolishly and write unthinking books. So the men who know that it is given to the mothers of earth to be very wise, stop their six part singing, or their jangles about the free-thinkers, and give attentive ear when Urda Bjarnason lights her pipe and begins her tale.

She is very old. Her daughters and sons are all dead, but her granddaughter, who is most respectable, and the cousin of a physician, says that Urda is twenty-four and a hundred, and there are others who say that she is older still. She watches all that the Iceland people do in the new land; she knows about the building of the five villages on the North Dakota plain, and of the founding of the churches and the schools, and the tilling of the wheat farms. She notes with suspicion the actions of the women who bring home webs of cloth from the store, instead of spinning them as their mothers did before them; and she shakes her head at the wives who run to the village grocery store every fortnight, imitating the wasteful American women, who throw butter in the fire faster than it can be turned from the churn.

She watches yet other things. All winter long the white snows reach across the gently rolling plains as far as the eye can behold.

In the morning she sees them tinted pink at the east; at noon she notes golden lights flashing across them; when the sky is gray—which is not often—she notes that they grow as ashen as a face with the death shadow on it. Sometimes they glitter with silver-like tips of ocean waves. But at these things she looks only casually. It is when the blue shadows dance on the snow that she leaves her corner behind the iron stove, and stands before the window, resting her two hands on the stout bar of her cane, and gazing out across the waste with eyes which age has restored after four decades of decrepitude.

The young Icelandmen say:

"Mother, it is the clouds hurrying across the sky that make the dance of the shadows."

"There are no clouds," she replies, and points to the jewel-like blue of the arching sky.

"It is the drifting air," explains Fridrik Halldersson, he who has been in the Northern seas. "As the wind buffets the air, it looks blue against the white of the snow. 'Tis the air that makes the dancing shadows."

But Urda shakes her head, and points with her dried finger, and those who stand beside her see figures moving, and airy shapes, and contortions of strange things, such as are seen in a beryl stone.

"But Urda Bjarnason," says Ingeborg Christianson, the pert young wife with the blue-eyed twins, "why is it we see these things only when we stand beside you and you help us to the sight?"

"Because," says the mother, with a steel-blue flash of her old eyes, "having eyes ye will not see!" Then the men laugh. They like to hear Ingeborg worsted. For did she not jilt two men from Gardar, and one from Mountain, and another from Winnipeg?

Not even Ingeborg can deny that Mother Urda tells true things.

"Today," says Urda, standing by the little window and watching the dance of the shadows, "a child breathed thrice on a farm at the West, and then it died."

71

The next week at the church gathering, when all the sledges stopped at the house of Urda's granddaughter, they said it was so—that John Christianson's wife Margaret never heard the voice of her son, but that he breathed thrice in his nurse's arms and died.

"Three sledges run over the snow toward Milton," says Urda; "all are laden with wheat, and in one is a stranger. He has with him a strange engine, but its purpose I do not know."

Six hours later the drivers of three empty sledges stop at the house.

"We have been to Milton with wheat," they say, "and Christian Johnson here, carried a photographer from St. Paul."

Now it stands to reason that the farmers like to amuse themselves through the silent and white winters. And they prefer above all things to talk or to listen, as has been the fashion of their race for a thousand years. Among all the story-tellers there is none like Urda, for she is the daughter and the granddaughter and the great-granddaughter of storytellers. It is given to her to talk, as it is given to John Thorlaksson to sing—he who sings so as his sledge flies over the snow at night, that the people come out in the bitter air from their doors to listen, and the dogs put up their noses and howl, not liking music.

In the little cabin of Peter Christianson, the husband of Urda's granddaughter, it sometimes happens that twenty men will gather about the stove. They hang their bear-skin coats on the wall, put their fur gauntlets underneath the stove, where they will keep warm, and then stretch their stout, felt-covered legs to the wood fire. The room is fetid; the coffee steams eternally on the stove; and from her chair in the warmest corner Urda speaks out to the listening men, who shake their heads with joy as they hear the pure old Icelandic flow in sweet rhythm from between her lips. Among the many, many tales she tells is that of the dead weaver, and she tells it in the simplest language in all the world—language so simple that even great scholars could find no simpler, and the children crawling on the floor can understand.

"Jon and Loa lived with their father and mother far to the north of the Island of Fire, and when the children looked from their windows they saw only wild scaurs and jagged lava rocks, and a distant, deep gleam of the sea. They caught the shine of the sea through an eye-shaped opening in the rocks, and all the long night of winter it gleamed up at them, like the eye of a dead witch. But when it sparkled and began to laugh, the children danced about the hut and sang, for they knew the bright summer time was at hand. Then their father fished, and their mother was gay. But it is true that even in the winter and the darkness they were happy, for they made fishing nets and baskets and cloth together,—Jon and Loa and their father and mother,—and the children were taught to read in the books, and were told the sagas, and given instruction in the part singing.

"They did not know there was such a thing as sorrow in the world, for no one had ever mentioned it to them. But one day their mother died. Then they had to learn how to keep the fire on the hearth, and to smoke the fish, and make the black coffee. And also they had to learn how to live when there is sorrow at the heart.

"They wept together at night for lack of their mother's kisses, and in the morning they were loath to rise because they could not see her face. The dead cold eye of the sea watching them from among the lava rocks made them afraid, so they hung a shawl over the window to keep it out. And the house, try as they would, did not look clean and cheerful as it had used to do when their mother sang and worked about it.

"One day, when a mist rested over the eye of the sea, like that which one beholds on the eyes of the blind, a greater sorrow came to them, for a stepmother crossed the threshold. She looked at Jon and Loa, and made complaint to their father that they were still very small and not likely to be of much use. After that they had to rise earlier than ever, and to work as only those who have their growth should work, till their hearts cracked for weariness and shame. They had not much to eat, for their stepmother said she would trust to the gratitude of no other woman's child, and that she believed in laying up against old age. So she put the few coins that came to the house in a strong box, and bought little food. Neither did she buy the children clothes, though those which their dear mother had made for them were so worn that the warp stood apart from the woof, and there were holes at the elbows and little warmth to be found in them anywhere.

"Moreover, the quilts on their beds were too short for their growing length, so that at night either their purple feet or their thin shoulders were uncovered, and they wept for the cold, and in the morning, when they crept into the larger room to build the fire, they were so stiff they could not stand straight, and there was pain at their joints.

"The wife scolded all the time, and her brow was like a storm sweeping down from the Northwest. There was no peace to be had in the house. The children might not repeat to each other the sagas their mother had taught them, nor try their part singing, nor make little doll cradles of rushes. Always they had to work, always they were scolded, always their clothes grew thinner.

"'Stepmother,' cried Loa one day,—she whom her mother had called the little bird,—'we are a-cold because of our rags. Our mother would have woven blue cloth for us and made it into garments.'

"'Your mother is where she will weave no cloth!' said the stepmother, and she laughed many times.

"All in the cold and still of that night, the stepmother wakened, and she knew not why. She sat up in her bed, and knew not why. She knew not why, and she looked into the room, and there, by the light of a burning fish's tail—'twas such a light the folk used in those days—was a woman, weaving. She had no loom, and shuttle she had none. All with her hands she wove a wondrous cloth. Stooping and bending, rising and swaying with motions beautiful as those the Northern Lights make in a midwinter sky, she wove a cloth. The warp was blue and mystical to see, the woof was white, and shone with its whiteness, so that of all the webs the stepmother had ever seen, she had seen none like to this.

"Yet the sight delighted her not, for beyond the drifting web, and beyond the weaver she saw the room and furniture—aye, saw them through the body of the weaver and the drifting of the cloth. Then she knew—as the haunted are made to know—that 'twas the mother of the children come to show her she could still weave cloth. The heart of the stepmother was cold as ice, yet she could not move to waken her husband at her side, for her hands were as fixed as if they were crossed on her dead breast. The voice in her was silent, and her tongue stood to the roof of her mouth.

"After a time the wraith of the dead mother moved toward her—the wraith of the weaver moved her way—and round and about her body was wound the shining cloth. Wherever it touched the body of the stepmother, it was as hateful to her as the touch of a monster out of sea-slime, so that her flesh crept away from it, and her senses swooned.

"In the early morning she awoke to the voices of the children, whispering in the inner room as they dressed with half-frozen fingers. Still about her was the hateful, beautiful web, filling her soul with loathing and with fear. She thought she saw the task set for her, and when the children crept in to light the fire—very purple and thin were their little bodies, and the rags hung from them—she arose and held out the shining cloth, and cried:

"'Here is the web your mother wove for you. I will make it into garments!' But even as she spoke the cloth faded and fell into nothingness, and the children cried:

"'Stepmother, you have the fever!'

"And then:

"'Stepmother, what makes the strange light in the room?'

"That day the stepmother was too weak to rise from her bed, and the children thought she must be going to die, for she did not scold as they cleared the house and braided their baskets, and she did not frown at them, but looked at them with wistful eyes.

"By fall of night she was as weary as if she had wept all the day, and so she slept. But again she was awakened and knew not why. And again she sat up in her bed and knew not why. And again, not knowing why, she looked and saw a woman weaving cloth. All that had happened the night before happened this night. Then, when the morning came, and the children crept in shivering from their beds, she arose and dressed herself, and from her strong box she took coins, and bade her husband go with her to the town.

"So that night a web of cloth, woven by one of the best weavers in all Iceland, was in the house; and on the beds of the children were blankets of lamb's wool, soft to the touch and fair to the eye. After that the children slept warm and were at peace; for now, when they told the sagas their mother had taught them, or tried their part songs as they sat together on their bench, the stepmother was silent. For she feared to chide, lest she should wake at night, not knowing why, and see the mother's wraith."

On the Northern Ice

The winter nights up at Sault Ste. Marie are as white and luminous as the Milky Way. The silence which rests upon the solitude appears to be white also. Even sound has been included in Nature's arrestment, for, indeed, save the still white frost, all things seem to be obliterated. The stars have a poignant brightness, but they belong to heaven and not to earth, and between their immeasurable height and the still ice rolls the ebon ether in vast, liquid billows.

In such a place it is difficult to believe that the world is actually peopled. It seems as if it might be the dark of the day after Cain killed Abel, and as if all of humanity's remainder was huddled in affright away from the awful spaciousness of Creation.

The night Ralph Hagadorn started out for Echo Bay—bent on a pleasant duty—he laughed to himself, and said that he did not at all object to being the only man in the world, so long as the world remained as unspeakably beautiful as it was when he buckled on his skates and shot away into the solitude. He was bent on reaching his best friend in time to act as groomsman, and business had delayed him till time was at its briefest. So he journeyed by night and journeyed alone, and when the tang of the frost got at his blood, he felt as a spirited horse feels when it gets free of bit and bridle. The ice was as glass, his skates were keen, his frame fit, and his venture to his taste! So he laughed, and cut through the air as a sharp stone cleaves the water. He could hear the whistling of the air as he cleft it.

As he went on and on in the black stillness, he began to have fancies. He imagined himself enormously tall—a great Viking of the Northland, hastening over icy fiords to his love. And that reminded him that he had a love—though, indeed, that thought was always present with him as a background for other thoughts. To be sure, he had not told her that she was his love, for he had seen her only a few times, and the auspicious occasion had not yet presented itself. She lived at Echo Bay also, and was to be the maid of honour to his friend's bride—which was one more reason why he skated almost as swiftly as the wind, and why, now and then, he let out a shout of exultation.

The one cloud that crossed Hagadorn's sun of expectancy was the knowledge that Marie Beaujeu's father had money, and that Marie lived in a house with two stories to it, and wore otter skin about her throat and little satin-lined mink boots on her feet when she went sledding. Moreover, in the locket in which she treasured a bit of her dead mother's hair, there was a black pearl as big as a pea. These things made it difficult—perhaps impossible—for Ralph Hagadorn to say more than, "I love you." But that much he meant to say though he were scourged with chagrin for his temerity.

This determination grew upon him as he swept along the ice under the starlight. Venus made a glowing path toward the west and seemed eager to reassure him. He was sorry he could not skim down that avenue of light which flowed from the love-star, but he was forced to turn his back upon it and face the black northeast.

It came to him with a shock that he was not alone. His eyelashes were frosted and his eyeballs blurred with the cold, so at first he thought it might be an illusion. But when he had rubbed his eyes hard, he made sure that not very far in front of him was a long white skater in fluttering garments who sped over the ice as fast as ever werewolf went.

He called aloud, but there was no answer. He shaped his hands and trumpeted through them, but the silence was as before—it was complete. So then he gave chase, setting his teeth hard and putting a tension on his firm young muscles. But go however he would, the white skater went faster. After a time, as he glanced at the cold gleam of the north star, he perceived that he was being led from his direct path. For a moment he hesitated, wondering if he would not better keep to his road, but his weird companion seemed to draw him on irresistibly, and finding it sweet to follow, he followed.

Of course it came to him more than once in that strange pursuit, that the white skater was no earthly guide. Up in those latitudes men see curious things when the hoar frost is on the earth. Hagadorn's own father—to hark no further than that for an instance!—who lived up there with the Lake Superior Indians, and worked in the copper mines, had welcomed a woman at his hut one bitter night, who was gone by morning, leaving wolf tracks on the snow! Yes, it was so, and John Fontanelle, the half-breed, could tell you about it any day—if he were alive. (Alack, the snow where the wolf tracks were, is melted now!)

Well, Hagadorn followed the white skater all the night, and when the ice flushed pink at dawn, and arrows of lovely light shot up into the cold heavens, she was gone, and Hagadorn was at his destination. The sun climbed arrogantly up to his place above all other things, and as Hagadorn took off his skates and glanced carelessly lakeward, he beheld a great wind-rift in the ice, and the waves showing blue and hungry between white fields. Had he rushed along his intended path, watching the stars to guide him, his glance turned upward, all his body at magnificent momentum, he must certainly have gone into that cold grave.

How wonderful that it had been sweet to follow the white skater, and that he followed!

His heart beat hard as he hurried to his friend's house. But he encountered no wedding furore. His friend met him as men meet in houses of mourning.

"Is this your wedding face?" cried Hagadorn. "Why, man, starved as I am, I look more like a bridegroom than you!"

"There's no wedding today!"

"No wedding! Why, you're not—"

"Marie Beaujeu died last night—"

"Marie—"

"Died last night. She had been skating in the afternoon, and she came home chilled and wandering in her mind, as if the frost had got in it somehow. She grew worse and worse, and all the time she talked of you."

"Of me?"

"We wondered what it meant. No one knew you were lovers."

"I didn't know it myself; more's the pity. At least, I didn't know—"

"She said you were on the ice, and that you didn't know about the big breaking-up, and she cried to us that the wind was off shore and the rift widening. She cried over and over again that you could come in by the old French creek if you only knew—"

"I came in that way."

"But how did you come to do that? It's out of the path. We thought perhaps—"

But Hagadorn broke in with his story and told him all as it had come to pass.

That day they watched beside the maiden, who lay with tapers at her head and at her feet, and in the little church the bride who might have been at her wedding said prayers for her friend. They buried Marie Beaujeu in her bridesmaid white, and Hagadorn was before the altar with her, as he had intended from the first! Then at midnight the lovers who were to wed whispered their vows in the gloom of the cold church, and walked together through the snow to lay their bridal wreaths upon a grave.

Three nights later, Hagadorn skated back again to his home. They wanted him to go by sunlight, but he had his way, and went when Venus made her bright path on the ice.

The truth was, he had hoped for the companionship of the white skater. But he did not have it. His only companion was the wind. The only voice he heard was the baying of a wolf on the north shore. The world was as empty and as white as if God had just created it, and the sun had not yet coloured nor man defiled it.

Story of an Obstinate Corpse

Virgil Hoyt is a photographer's assistant up at St. Paul, and enjoys his work without being consumed by it. He has been in search of the picturesque all over the West and hundreds of miles to the north, in Canada, and can speak three or four Indian dialects and put a canoe through the rapids. That is to say, he is a man of adventure, and no dreamer. He can fight well and shoot better, and swim so as to put up a winning race with the Indian boys, and he can sit in the saddle all day and not worry about it tomorrow.

Wherever he goes, he carries a camera.

"The world," Hoyt is in the habit of saying to those who sit with him when he smokes his pipe, "was created in six days to be photographed. Man—and particularly woman—was made for the same purpose. Clouds are not made to give moisture nor trees to cast shade. They have been created in order to give the camera obscura something to do."

In short, Virgil Hoyt's view of the world is whimsical, and he likes to be bothered neither with the disagreeable nor the mysterious. That is the reason he loathes and detests going to a house of mourning to photograph a corpse. The bad taste of it offends him, but above all, he doesn't like the necessity of shouldering, even for a few moments, a part of the burden of sorrow which belongs to some one else. He dislikes sorrow, and would willingly canoe five hundred miles up the cold Canadian rivers to get rid of it. Nevertheless, as assistant photographer, it is often his duty to do this very kind of thing.

Not long ago he was sent for by a rich Jewish family to photograph the remains of the mother, who had just died. He was put out, but he was only an assistant, and he went. He was taken to the front parlour, where the dead woman lay in her coffin. It was evident to him that there was some excitement in the household, and that a discussion was going on. But Hoyt said to himself that it didn't concern him, and he therefore paid no attention to it.

The daughter wanted the coffin turned on end in order that the corpse might face the camera properly, but Hoyt said he could overcome the recumbent attitude and make it appear that the face was taken in the position it would naturally hold in life, and so they went out and left him alone with the dead.

The face of the deceased was a strong and positive one, such as may often be seen among Jewish matrons. Hoyt regarded it with some admiration, thinking to himself that she was a woman who had known what she wanted, and who, once having made up her mind, would prove immovable. Such a character appealed to Hoyt. He reflected that he might have married if only he could have found a woman with strength of character sufficient to disagree with him. There was a strand of hair out of place on the dead woman's brow, and he gently pushed it back. A bud lifted its head too high from among the roses on her breast and spoiled the contour of the chin, so he broke it off. He remembered these things later with keen distinctness, and that his hand touched her chill face two or three times in the making of his arrangements.

Then he took the impression, and left the house.

He was busy at the time with some railroad work, and several days passed before he found opportunity to develop the plates. He took them from the bath in which they had lain with a number of others, and went energetically to work upon them, whistling some very saucy songs he had learned of the guide in the Red River country, and trying to forget that the face which was presently to appear was that of a dead woman. He had used three plates as a precaution against accident, and they came up well. But as they developed, he became aware of the existence of something in the photograph which had not been apparent to his eye in the subject. He was irritated, and without attempting to face the mystery, he made a few prints and laid them aside, ardently hoping that by some chance they would never be called for.

However, as luck would have it,—and Hoyt's luck never had been good,—his employer asked one day what had become of those photographs. Hoyt tried to evade making an answer, but the effort was futile, and he had to get out the finished prints and exhibit them. The older man sat staring at them a long time.

"Hoyt," he said, "you're a young man, and very likely you have never seen anything like this before. But I have. Not exactly the same thing, perhaps, but similar phenomena have come my way a number of times since I went in the business, and I want to tell you there are things in heaven and earth not dreamt of—"

"Oh, I know all that tommy-rot," cried Hoyt, angrily, "but when anything happens I want to know the reason why and how it is done."

"All right," answered his employer, "then you might explain why and how the sun rises."

But he humoured the young man sufficiently to examine with him the baths in which the plates were submerged, and the plates themselves. All was as it should be; but the mystery was there, and could not be done away with.

Hoyt hoped against hope that the friends of the dead woman would somehow forget about the photographs; but the idea was unreasonable, and one day, as a matter of course, the daughter appeared and asked to see the pictures of her mother.

"Well, to tell the truth," stammered Hoyt, "they didn't come out quite—quite as well as we could wish."

"But let me see them," persisted the lady. "I'd like to look at them anyhow."

"Well, now," said Hoyt, trying to be soothing, as he believed it was always best to be with women,—to tell the truth he was an ignoramus where women were concerned,—"I think it would be better if you didn't look at them. There are reasons why—" he ambled on like this, stupid man that he was, till the lady naturally insisted upon seeing the pictures without a moment's delay.

So poor Hoyt brought them out and placed them in her hand, and then ran for the water pitcher, and had to be at the bother of bathing her forehead to keep her from fainting.

For what the lady saw was this: Over face and flowers and the head of the coffin fell a thick veil, the edges of which touched the floor in some places. It covered the features so well that not a hint of them was visible.

"There was nothing over mother's face!" cried the lady at length.

"Not a thing," acquiesced Hoyt. "I know, because I had occasion to touch her face just before I took the picture. I put some of her hair back from her brow."

"What does it mean, then?" asked the lady.

"You know better than I. There is no explanation in science. Perhaps there is some in—in psychology."

"Well," said the young woman, stammering a little and colouring, "mother was a good woman, but she always wanted her own way, and she always had it, too."

"Yes."

"And she never would have her picture taken. She didn't admire her own appearance. She said no one should ever see a picture of her."

"So?" said Hoyt, meditatively. "Well, she's kept her word, hasn't she?"

The two stood looking at the photographs for a time. Then Hoyt pointed to the open blaze in the grate.

"Throw them in," he commanded. "Don't let your father see them—don't keep them yourself. They wouldn't be agreeable things to keep."

"That's true enough," admitted the lady. And she threw them in the fire. Then Virgil Hoyt brought out the plates and broke them before her eyes.

And that was the end of it—except that Hoyt sometimes tells the story to those who sit beside him when his pipe is lighted.

Story of the Vanishing Patient

There had always been strange stories about the house, but it was a sensible, comfortable sort of a neighbourhood, and people took pains to say to one another that there was nothing in these tales—of course not! Absolutely nothing! How could there be? It was a matter of common remark, however, that considering the amount of money the Nethertons had spent on the place, it was curious they lived there so little. They were nearly always away,—up North in the summer and down South in the winter, and over to Paris or London now and then,—and when they did come home it was only to entertain a number of guests from the city. The place was either plunged in gloom or gayety. The old gardener who kept house by himself in the cottage at the back of the yard had things much his own way by far the greater part of the time.

Dr. Block and his wife lived next door to the Nethertons, and he and his wife, who were so absurd as to be very happy in each other's company, had the benefit of the beautiful yard. They walked there mornings when the leaves were silvered with dew, and evenings they sat beside the lily pond and listened for the whip-poor-will. The doctor's wife moved her room over to that side of the house which commanded a view of the yard, and thus made the honeysuckles and laurel and clematis and all the masses of tossing greenery her own. Sitting there day after day with her sewing, she speculated about the mystery which hung impalpably yet undeniably over the house.

It happened one night when she and her husband had gone

to their room, and were congratulating themselves on the fact that he had no very sick patients and was likely to enjoy a good night's rest, that a ring came at the door.

"If it's anyone wanting you to leave home," warned his wife, "you must tell them you are all worn out. You've been disturbed every night this week, and it's too much!"

The young physician went downstairs. At the door stood a man whom he had never seen before.

"My wife is lying very ill next door," said the stranger, "so ill that I fear she will not live till morning. Will you please come to her at once?"

"Next door?" cried the physician. "I didn't know the Nethertons were home!"

"Please hasten," begged the man. "I must go back to her. Follow as quickly as you can."

The doctor went back upstairs to complete his toilet.

"How absurd," protested his wife when she heard the story. "There is no one at the Nethertons'. I sit where I can see the front door, and no one can enter without my knowing it, and I have been sewing by the window all day. If there were any one in the house, the gardener would have the porch lantern lighted. It is some plot. Someone has designs on you. You must not go."

But he went. As he left the room his wife placed a revolver in his pocket.

The great porch of the mansion was dark, but the physician made out that the door was open, and he entered. A feeble light came from the bronze lamp at the turn of the stairs, and by it he found his way, his feet sinking noiselessly in the rich carpets. At the head of the stairs the man met him. The doctor thought himself a tall man, but the stranger topped him by half a head. He motioned the physician to follow him, and the two went down the hall to the front room. The place was flushed with a rose-colored glow from several lamps. On a silken couch, in the midst of pillows, lay a woman dying with consumption. She was like a lily, white, shapely, graceful, with feeble yet charming movements. She looked at the doctor appealingly, then, seeing in his eyes the involuntary verdict that her hour was at hand, she turned toward her companion with a glance of anguish. Dr. Block asked a few questions. The man answered them, the woman remaining silent. The physician administered something stimulating, and then wrote a prescription which he placed on the mantel-shelf.

"The drug store is closed tonight," he said, "and I fear the druggist has gone home. You can have the prescription filled the first thing in the morning, and I will be over before breakfast."

After that, there was no reason why he should not have gone home. Yet, oddly enough, he preferred to stay. Nor was it professional anxiety that prompted this delay. He longed to watch those mysterious persons, who, almost oblivious of his presence, were speaking their mortal farewells in their glances, which were impassioned and of unutterable sadness.

He sat as if fascinated. He watched the glitter of rings on the woman's long, white hands, he noted the waving of light hair about her temples, he observed the details of her gown of soft white silk which fell about her in voluminous folds. Now and then the man gave her of the stimulant which the doctor had provided; sometimes he bathed her face with water. Once he paced the floor for a moment till a motion of her hand quieted him.

After a time, feeling that it would be more sensible and considerate of him to leave, the doctor made his way home. His wife was awake, impatient to hear of his experiences. She listened to his tale in silence, and when he had finished she turned her face to the wall and made no comment.

"You seem to be ill, my dear," he said. "You have a chill. You are shivering."

"I have no chill," she replied sharply. "But I—well, you may leave the light burning."

The next morning before breakfast the doctor crossed the dewy sward to the Netherton house. The front door was locked, and no one answered to his repeated ringings. The old gardener chanced to be cutting the grass near at hand, and he came running up.

"What you ringin' that door-bell for, doctor?" said he. "The folks ain't come home yet. There ain't nobody there."

"Yes, there is, Jim. I was called here last night. A man came for me to attend his wife. They must both have fallen asleep that the bell is not answered. I wouldn't be surprised to find her dead, as a matter of fact. She was a desperately sick woman. Perhaps she is dead and something has happened to him. You have the key to the door, Jim. Let me in."

But the old man was shaking in every limb, and refused to do as he was bid.

"Don't you never go in there, doctor," whispered he, with chattering teeth. "Don't you go for to 'tend no one. You jus' come tell me when you sent for that way. No, I ain't goin' in, doctor, nohow. It ain't part of my duties to go in. That's been stipulated by Mr. Netherton. It's my business to look after the garden."

Argument was useless. Dr. Block took the bunch of keys from the old man's pocket and himself unlocked the front door and entered. He mounted the steps and made his way to the upper room. There was no evidence of occupancy. The place was silent, and, so far as living creature went, vacant. The dust lay over everything. It covered the delicate damask of the sofa where he had seen the dying woman. It rested on the pillows. The place smelled musty and evil, as if it had not been used for a long time. The lamps of the room held not a drop of oil.

But on the mantel-shelf was the prescription which the doctor had written the night before. He read it, folded it, and put it in his pocket.

As he locked the outside door the old gardener came running to him.

"Don't you never go up there again, will you?" he pleaded, "not unless you see all the Nethertons home and I come for you myself. You won't, doctor?"

"No," said the doctor.

When he told his wife she kissed him, and said:

90

"Next time when I tell you to stay at home, you must stay!"

The Angel With the Broom

Paula Landless walked slowly down the street looking for a home, as any discerning person might almost have surmised, so wide and examining were her eyes, so wistful and importunate her mouth, so pallid and lonely her face.

The discerning person would not have said that Paula Landless was young. At least, not quite. She had been young perhaps, last year, or the year before that, when she lived in her Iowa home, and had known next to nothing of life. The home, swarming with girls, had crowded her out; the old sad world had called to her. She had felt very strong and full of pity, and so had come up to Chicago, where a number of things were going badly, to help set them aright. For two years she had attended a school with a long and imposing name, and had come out to join the great army of welfare workers who insist that if you try hard enough, you can make almost everybody happy. Paula, now a member of a certain society of combined—one had almost said syndicated—charities, was as said before, looking for a home.

She wanted it to be among "her people," her unconscious and probably protesting parishioners; she was bent passionately upon the idea of "neighbouring," and it was necessary therefore, to find a home in the very "midst of things." This being in the midst of things meant being in the midst of much squalor and dirt, many children and innumerable germs, it seemed. Paula had looked at many rooms that morning that turned her squeamish, and had reproached herself for being disgustingly fastidious, a provincial Pharisee, a snob, a hypocrite. She quite exhausted herself with the hurling of self-reproachful epithets. But in spite of all this, she had edged, little by little, onto a cleaner street.

It was a curious street; not littered precisely, for the pavement was clean; but cluttered rather with little shops; little insistent shops that made their nature at once known, and that somehow cried out the personality as well as the nationality of their owners. There a Russian, here a German, across the way an Italian, yonder a Bohemian. Oh, and beyond a Polish midwife, next to an Irish undertaker; and all in between and round about saloons, as cosmopolitan as sin.

If the summer day had not been darkening for a shower, Paula could have seen much better. As it was, she had to go rather close to the little shops and peer into them, hoping she might see some "room for rent" sign which would give her an excuse to rest her weary feet.

So that was how, peering in what seemed the darkest of them all, she beheld a sight not to be forgotten. A girl, ten years of age perhaps, slender and spiritual, with black eyes and a torrent of black curls, stood in the shaft of light that fell from an overhanging lamp, holding high two seven-branched candlesticks of ancient beaten brass. Her scant white dress clung about her slender limbs, and her long, uncovered arms trembled with the weight of the candelabra. She looked as if about to take flight, all radiant and white and delicate as she was, and Paula stopped, her breath caught in her throat, wondering how, amid so much ugliness, a thing of beauty like this should be.

Then she saw the child's surroundings—saw too, the meaning of her gesture. A man, her father, no doubt, stood on the counter above her, arranging his wares on the shelf. And such wares! Candlesticks old and new, basins and pitchers of brass and amalgam, samovars, fire irons, stewpans of copper, bells of bronze. Then on other shelves, books in an inviting array; books done in vellum with clasps of brass or of silver; other books in tongues that flung their cabalistic titles sardonically at Paula's ignorance; heaped pamphlets in equally strange letters.

"Oh!" said Paula softly, clasping her hands in their shabby gloves. And then again: "Oh!"

"You want something, Miss?" asked the man on the counter.

Paula looked up at him and smiled. He was small, dark and eager with an eagle-like nose and eyes as bright as his daughter's.

"I want," said Paula, "A—a home." She paused; then said: "If you please."

"A home?" He seemed puzzled, but he looked nicely human, and amenable to neighbourly offices.

"Yes. A room, you know. I must live hereabouts. I'm going to work for the Amalgamated Charities. I'd like to be—to be near here."

Moses Lubin knew she was polite by what she did not say. He took the candlesticks from his daughter, placed them on a shelf and jumped down from the counter.

"Mama, mama," he called. "Here is a young miss who wants a home."

Then Paula met Mrs. Lubin, who was little too, and dark, and looked as if she might sometime have shed terrible tears. She took Paula in swiftly; and as swiftly made up her mind when Paula had told her tale.

"I have a good neighbour who will take you," she said. "She will be glad."

The good neighbour lived next door. Mrs. Hunding, wife of Otto Hunding, the stationer and tobacconist. Germans—blond, broad, kindly and willing to make a little more than expenses.

Yes, they had a room—the front upstairs room. Unfurnished. Paula looked at it. Three windows with small panes looked out on the thronged street. The floor was new; the paper clean and not so bright a green as one might have feared.

"Would you be willing to be a little social, evenings?" asked Mrs. Hunding, looking at Paula with maternal eyes.

"Oh, yes, certainly. I should love it. I—I am all alone in the city, Mrs. Hunding. It is very good of you—"

Mrs. Hunding raised a large deprecatory hand.

"It is not good of me," she said succinctly. "I wish it—for my son."

Suddenly her lips quivered. Paula drew a little closer to her.

"I am afraid I don't quite understand."

"My son is not well. He goes nowhere. But he is very bright. He would have been a fine man already only—"

She paused.

"Let me see him," said the girl who meant to set things right.

Frau Hunding led the way to a little alcove which opened off the main part of the shop, commanding a tiny window that inserted itself unobtrusively between the show windows of the Hunding and the Lubin shops. Here, in his invalid's chair sat a young man, blue of eye, mild of countenance, with a dreamer's head and ripe lips which life had failed to touch to sensuality. There was a look of ineptitude about him—the look of a youth hopelessly defeated. Paula's eyes swept him involuntarily as if to learn the meaning of this expression. She saw then that his legs were shrivelled, and that he was as useless as a rag doll for all the practical purposes of life.

His eyes besought her favour, timorously and yet proudly like a child's eyes. She found herself holding out her hand:

"Your mother says I may live here," she said brightly. "And that evenings I may sit with the family." Her voice faltered a little, from pitying embarrassment. "You play chess?" she asked, groping for some union of tastes.

So she became, in a way, one of them. She put a cot, a deal table, three chairs and an alarm clock in the bare room above the shop. She had enough bedclothes for cleanliness and almost enough for warmth. Mrs. Hunding set a blooming plant in the room; Mrs. Lubin contributed a brass inkwell. From her trunk Paula unearthed a little handworked table spread, and some photographs of the home folk. She was settled then and quite content, and she went about her work very bravely, very eagerly. All day she laboured among the poor, the foreign, the ill. And her heart sang within, because she thought she was setting things right—because she believed that by and by she and the others who worked with her, would get ahead of the misery, would ride through it, so to speak, and come out on the other side.

Then, nights, the Hundings heard the stories of her adventures, and the blue eyes of Casper Hunding shone upon her in understanding.

"I told you, Hunding, that it would he a good thing for Casper to have the maiden here," Frau Hunding whispered to her husband when Paula had been with them a week. "You see for yourself how it is. He laughs with her; he beats her at chess; never have I seen him so happy."

But Hunding shook his big head.

"Today, yes," he said. "But what comes tomorrow?"

"Maybe," said Frau Hunding sharply, "there will not be very many tomorrows for my boy already."

If the Hundings and the Lubins had liked each other well enough before, they became true friends now. The little welfare worker drew them together. She flashed from one place to the other with her golden gossip, telling each pleasant things of the other. She sewed on doll dresses for little Miriam Lubin, who stole in evenings to hang over her chair and listen to her stories of what was to be found out in the world. Miriam danced for the Hundings, who thought her like a fairy, and sometimes Casper and Miriam and Paula sang together the more melodious of the street songs that were forever making their way into the neighbourhood. And while they were singing Moses Lubin and his wife and the two elder Hundings would sit outside and listen, feeling more at home than they had done since they left their own countries.

It was now a pleasure for Lubin to go into Hunding's shop each morning and evening, calling out:

"My paper, if you please, neighbour."

"Here it is, laid aside for you, neighbour." They talked over the news together, feeling like allies; like men with a common experience, both being from the old country. They meant to be good to each other if trouble ever came. The homesickness that had been forever like a shadow in their hearts began to grow less. They felt settled at last. They loved to watch little Miriam, who was so happy and so unspotted from the world; they were all tender with Casper, doomed in his youth; they had a reverence for the eager, white faced Paula Landless, who was like Elizabeth of Hungary, or Catherine of Siena. Hunding made the comparisons. Lubin did not object to them. He, too, believed in saints.

Then the morning came when Lubin, going in for his paper, lingered a little longer than was his wont.

This is news for you," said Hunding.

The Archduke of Austria has been slain by an assassin. The work of a revolutionist, no doubt. I have my opinion of these revolutionists, Lubin, and I cannot see how it is that a man like you will sell their dirty pamphlets."

"I have no dirty pamphlets in my place, neighbour. On the contrary, I keep the books of the highest thinkers—social democrats, syndicalists, sabotists, the Industrial Workers of the World, the intellectuals of Russia—all sorts. You do not understand this ferment, neighbour."

"And to what does it lead, Lubin? Answer me that? To murder,—to—"

"A king more or less does not trouble me, Hunding. This archduke was a dangerous man; he was against the cause of liberty—" his voice began to rise. Casper over in his alcove, felt a trembling creep over his body. He could not endure raised voices.

"Father, father," he called, "I am not well. Would you bring me some cold water?"

Lubin went home and a little later Mrs. Lubin came over with some broth for Casper.

"What good neighbours we have. Otto," said Mrs. Hunding. "What do you two care about kings or revolutionists? Keep your shops and hold your tongues."

Hunding agreed. He apologized to Lubin. Lubin accepted his view.

97

"We are both good men," said they to themselves, each after his own fashion, and thinking in his own tongue. "What reason have we to quarrel?"

But overseas other good men were quarrelling. They were being driven forth from their little, contented homes, from their little busy shops. They who had been so harmlessly occupied in the gentler tasks of living, were being forced to an ultimate task. Their manhood was being tried out by the last test. They, who had no hate, were being educated in it; they whose hands were bloodless, were receiving instructions in the red art of war. Day by day the horror grew, as "the far-flung battle line" stretched out across stricken miles; as beautiful towns lay in ruins; as valleys and rivers were heaped with the dead; as the smoke of funeral pyres lifted from devastated fields.

Those in the struggle arose to the hour; those far from it felt their hearts bleed with a vicarious anguish greater than they could express. It seemed the catastrophe of civilisation; the vast disillusionment of a world which had dreamed of brotherhood.

And now Hunding knew himself for a German indeed, and the loyal subject of his emperor; and Lubin, loving no emperor, with no cause to love his country, palpitated to Russia's name with every drop of blood in his dark little body. With each German advance, Hunding swelled with a pride that was more than a pride. It was more than love of country. It was the very essence of his manhood. And as the *Czar's* vast armies mobilised, ever pouring in from their remote homes, all that was wild and free, strong and sad, stirred in the passionate breast of Lubin as the forces of a burning mountain leap in its deep heart.

"Hah, Germany, Germany, my Fatherland!" cried Hunding one morning. "It is not afraid to be misunderstood. It stands between the hordes of the East guarding and protecting the world. What does it care for scorn? Germany does her duty to the end."

"Madness! Madness!" shrieked Lubin. "Your warlord, your blood sucker, who calls a treaty a little piece of paper! Shame on you that you honour such a man! Shame on the men that follow him to battle, to wade in blood and tears!"

Casper in his alcove, put his face in his hands. He could not stand to see little Miriam dancing without on the pavement to the sound of a hurdy-gurdy, she so joyous, and these fathers so swollen with anger. He longed for Paula Landless who knew how to speak words of peace. As for him, he could not speak. He felt faint again. The world was going round—going round. Hunding had come out from behind his counter, and towered over Lubin, who backed toward the door. Then Casper, through the blur of his senses saw them both to be on the sidewalk, saw Miriam standing with both hands to her mouth as if in fright.

Next the neighbours came running—La Vergne, the barber, Latta, the fruit man, Copal, the saloon keeper, Mrs. Wittowsky, the midwife. And others. Many others. They all came running. They stood on tiptoe to see and hear. They backed Hunding; they backed Lubin. And presently all were talking, gesticulating, threatening, calling on their countries, on their emperors, on their God, each in his own tongue, each for the glory of the Quarrel that was shaking the world.

So Mahony, the policeman, thought best to turn in a call for the capacious blue wagon, for see you, Latta had a knife and Copal a pistol, and Lubin was tearing his beard with an immemorial gesture—and the hurdy-gurdy was playing *The Watch On the Rhine*.

That was how Hunding and Lubin and Latta and La Vergne and all the rest of them came to be arrested for disturbing the peace. Thrown together in the general cell, they fumed and sorrowed and suffered and raged according to their temperaments, and if it had not been for an alderman of paternal habits and a copious—one had almost said a communal—purse, they would have fared worse than they did. It was bad enough as it was, considering that they were honest men, and men of self-respect.

As for their women who watched them being driven away, they would have taken up the fight and been glad to do it, for their blood was boiling and their affections were wounded in their tenderest spot, had it not been that little Miriam, a quivering spectator, chanced to look within the alcove where Casper sat. She saw that his head was lying back against the chair, that his eyes were rolling, and his face strangely flushed.

"Casper!" she cried so shrilly that Anna Hunding, his mother, heard and looked and ran.

"Ah, you kill him among you!" she accused.

But he was not dead. He came back to life intensely, tremendously, with gleaming eyes, with parted lips as one who beheld a vision.

Then he spoke, strangely, like one chanting, and the neighbours, crowding around, stood spell-bound to hear.

"Mother," he called, "Mother."

"Casper, my boy!"

"Do you hear them marching? Do you hear the men marching? Hear their footsteps? Hear the drum beats? It keeps saying: '*Fear-fear, fear-fear, fear-fear!* Fear of Russians, fear of Germans, fear of English, fear of French.' Hear it beating? What a drum-beat! *Fear-fear!* Don't let father join them, mother. Don't let neighbour Lubin go. See them coming—see them coming? Miles and miles of men all marching. Miles and more miles. 'Pride-pride, pride-pride, pride of Russians, pride of Germans, pride of English, pride of French.' Hear the drum beats—"

He had spoken the words as if to the deep pulsation of a drum. But now a new expression crossed his face. He shrank back in his chair as if to avoid the very scrutiny of God, and when his mother rushed to him he held her back.

"Keep away, keep away!" he cried. "Give them room, mother, give them room."

"Give who room, my boy? Oh, what do you see?"

"Angels, mother, fighting, fighting. The angel in purple is the Angel of Pride, and the one in grey is the Angel of Fear. Oh, what terrible faces they have! I do not know which is worse. Ah-aa-aa, how they struggle. Oh, mother, they need all the world to fight in. See the towns fall to give them room. Ah-aa-" He sank back weakly. The strange and terrible elation faded from his face, and he looked at his mother with blurred eyes.

"I am very tired," he said, letting her take his hands. "Has Paula come home yet?"

When Paula did come and heard all the tale, she looked at Casper with awe. The mother saw it and turned her head away. Did it mean he was near his end, that he, so many years her babe, her care, her joy-in-sorrow, was leaving her? Was his vision the forerunner of his death?

Like a maiden of snow, Paula sat by his chair, listening and weeping, nor would she be comforted till the crestfallen men came home and sullenly took up their work again.

After that, Lubin came no more for his paper. Paula carried it over and dropped it at his door; or Miriam, softly entering the white conspiracy stole into Hunding's for it. When the Lubins passed the Hundings there were averted looks. No little dishes of soup were now sent from next door to strengthen the sick boy. If Paula took Miriam to a party at the Settlement house, she did not tell the Hundings where she was going. The men had been warned and they kept the peace, but as the paper brought each morning the news of the on-sweep of the European tragedy, each knew what the other was thinking, and to each his neighbours' expletives seemed to hiss behind the door like cornered snakes.

As for Paula, she drooped. The clash of temperaments thrust her into a place of doubt and dread where she lost sight of that Perfect Good toward which she was working. She grew paler, thinner; her little hands were habitually cold; her eyes grew larger in her wistful face. She was growing used to seeing hungry people, and drunken people, and people who were sinners, and people who were about to die. She could stand that. It was her business to stand it. But the Lubins and the Hundings were somehow her own. With her great talent for loving, she loved them, and when their hates clashed, she shrunk as if from open blows. Besides, she knew in the quivering soul of her that Casper suffered from it even more than she.

"Men, men!" sighed Mrs. Hunding to her. "They are so fierce and wild! Always fighting yet for this idea and that! 'What's the matter with you at all,' I say to Hunding. 'You, with your ideas. Leave ideas alone. Be happy. In a little while you will be dead.' Here is Christmas coming, and what good will it do us with our hearts all black with hate? I wanted to make a pudding for the Lubins. I don't care if they are not Christians. They would have liked a pudding at Christmas as well as anyone. They would know it spoke of the friendship of our hearts. That is what I said to myself. But now what do we send them? Black looks; angry thoughts; whisperings and nudgings. Men, men!"

"Well," declared Paula with her downright Iowa determination, "no man has any say about what I shall do, and I intend to dress a new doll for Miriam. If the men want to be stupid that's their affair, but I'll not have a sweet little girl cheated of her Christmas."

"Maybe her father will let her take a present from you," sighed Frau Hunding, "but it would be useless for me to try to give her anything. I am their enemy. Oh, of course, their enemy!"

"You never could be the enemy of anyone," protested Paula, putting her slim arm about her protector's copious waist. "How can I thank you for being so good to me, mother Hunding?"

Sadder and more terrible grew the news from over seas. Darker and more cruel were the looks which Otto Hunding and Moses Lubin exchanged. So what pleasure was there to be found in sitting up late o'nights sewing on Christmas presents? How was the kindly spirit of Christmas to grope its way through the grey mist which hung over the place?

Then a day came—it must have been less than a week before Christmas—when Casper, very pale, very inert, sat listening against his will while his father read terrible stories of week-long battles, of driven and desperate men, of rivers choked with the slain. Casper, shrinking from the words as if they were blows, grew paler yet and cried out to his father to stop, but could not make his voice heard. Then as the vision of these innocent men, made murderous against their better natures, arose before him— these men dying in trenches, in the fields they had sown, or on the hard stones of foreign town—once more black confusion swirled in his brain. Again he sank into unconsciousness. It was a chance visitor to the shop who noticed it first.

"Has the young man fainted?" he asked.

Mrs. Hunding and Paula ran together toward the invalid, but before they could reach him his eyelids fluttered and he seemed to be struggling up through waves of deep oblivion to the light of exaltation. As on the previous occasion, his face was transfigured. His eyes were lit with a heavenly glory, his mouth bowed itself like a seraph's; but this time there was no dread, no pain. He was uplifted by the cognizance of some perfect beauty.

"He has come!" he chanted. "I have waited long, but he has come!"

"Oh, who, Casper, please?" asked Paula, looking where he looked and trying to see with his eyes. "Who?"

"The Angel," he answered. "The shining Angel—the white Angel. Oh, call our neighbours. They must see! Hasten, call them. They must see."

"Yes," said Paula, tranced with his vision, though she saw it not.

She sped next door, trembling, white-faced.

"Casper needs you," she cried. "Come!He has sent for you."

"By the faith of my father's I will not go," cried Lubin.

But Paula did not listen. She took his arm in her grasp.

"He is seeing an Angel," she cried. "And he wants you to see it too."

"Oh! Oh, an Angel!" said little Miriam. She dropped her toys and sped ahead. Mrs. Lubin had already gone on swift feet.

"Is he dying then?" she asked.

"Come, come," the youth called to them as they entered. "It is for you to see, and you will tell the others. See how it fills the room with its wings brighter than silver clouds. See its face, like the smile of God. And behold with your eyes what it is doing. It is sweeping away the landmarks with its shining broom. Do you understand? Sweeping away all that holds man from man. Down go boundaries! Down go divisions! No more Russian lines, no more German lines, no more French, Austrian and Italian lines.

All gone, wiped out. Do you understand? Just men, men, men, living, loving, laughing, working, helping! Just men with no lines between them! And the kings walking with the rest, men too, and shouting with joy because of the Angel with the broom." He is a prophet,'" said Moses Lubin, and stroked his beard.

"He is a saint," said Hunding. "My son, and I a sinner!"

Suddenly the youth flung his arm across his eyes.

"Mother!" he screamed. "It is too bright! I cannot stand the radiance! Oh, what wings—what wings."

Mrs. Hunding dropped her face in her hands. She dared not approach him. It was little Miriam who went to him.

"Don't be afraid, Casper," she whispered. "Nothing is too bright. Nothing is ever too bright."

He looked at her, dazed.

"Where am I?" he cried. Then he saw the familiar room, the familiar faces—saw Lubin and Mrs. Lubin, and he caught Miriam to him.

"Are you back?" he asked. "Are you our neighbours again?"

His eyes, purer than a child's, blue with the blueness like a June day, begged for their understanding.

Otto Hunding strode to Moses Lubin.

"In the name of God," he said, holding out his hand.

"In the name of God," said Lubin, grasping it

Mrs. Hunding caught the faded purple skirt of Mrs. Lubin with her trembling hand.

"I may send you my pudding on Christmas day?" she faltered. "I may give my little gift to Miriam?"

"Oh, yes, yes," said Rachel Lubin weeping. "Now I feel happy again. Now I feel once more as if I was at home."

Paula had an idea. She explored the recesses of the worn brown wrist bag which the children of her street knew to their pleasure, and drew forth some small objects. With these she went first to the giant Hunding, slipping something in his buttonhole; then to little Lubin and fastened something in his. Each man turned the lapel of his coat to see what she had done.

"Peace," read the little buttons. "Peace."

They looked at each other with penitent eyes, not ill at ease, yet not themselves. The place still was filled with the rustle of the wings of Casper's Angel; they seemed to hear the swish of his shining broom, sweeping away the landmarks. They were as folk who had partaken of a sacrament.

Casper's face was wistful now, like a tired child's, but his eyes continued to look like crystal pools. Beside him was Miriam, her dark hair streaming across his shoulder.

"Tomorrow," said Paula, seeking for some subject of conversation to break the spell that held them, "will be Christmas day."

Casper sat up in his chair and lifted his transparent hand.

"Peace day," he cried, "goodwill day!"

"Amen," said Hunding.

"*Selah*," said Lubin.

The Blood Apple
(A.k.a. *The Curse of Micah Rood*)

In the early part of the last century there lived in eastern
Connecticut a man named Micah Rood. He was a solitary soul,
and occupied a low, tumble-down house, in which he had seen
his sisters and his brothers, his father and his mother, die. The
mice used the bare floors for a playground; the swallows filled up
the unused chimneys; and in the attic a hundred bats made their
home. Micah Rood disturbed no living creature, unless now and
then he killed a hare for his day's dinner, or cast bait for a glistening trout in the Shetucket. For the most part his food came
from the garden and the orchard which his father had planted
and nurtured years before.

Into whatever disrepair the house had fallen, the garden
bloomed and flourished like a western Eden. The brambles, with
their luscious burden, clambered up the stone walls, sentinelled
by trim rows of English currants. The strawberry nestled among
its wayward creepers, and on the trellises hung grapes of varied
hues. In seemly rows, down the sunny expanse of the garden
spot, grew every vegetable indigenous to the western world or
transplanted by colonial industry. Everything here took seed,
and bore fruit with a prodigal exuberance. Beyond the garden
lay the orchard, a labyrinth of flowers in the springtime, a para-
dise of verdure in the summer, and in the season of fruition a
miracle of plenty.

Often the master of the orchard stood by the gate in the
crisp autumn mornings, with his hat filled with apples for the

children as they passed to school. There was only one tree in the orchard of whose fruit he was chary. Consequently it was the bearings of this tree that the children most wanted.

"Prithee, Master Rood," they would say, "give us some of the gold apples?"

"I sell the gold apples for siller," he would say. "Content ye with the red and green ones."

In all the region there grew no counterpart to this remarkable apple. Its skin was of the clearest amber, translucent and spotless, and the pulp was white as snow, mellow yet firm, and without a flaw from the glistening skin to the even, brown seeds nestling like babies in their silken cradle. Its flavour was peculiar and piquant, with a suggestion of spiciness. The fame of Micah Rood's apple, as it was called, had extended far and wide, but all efforts to engraft it upon other trees failed utterly; and the envious farmers were fain to content themselves with the rare shoots.

If there dwelt any vanity in the heart of Micah Rood, it was in the possession of this apple tree, which took the prize at all the local fairs and carried his name beyond the neighbourhood where its owner lived. For the most part he was a modest man, averse to discussions of any sort, shrinking from men and their opinions. He talked more to his dog than to any human being. He fed his mind upon a few old books, and made nature his religion. All things that made the woods their home were his friends. He possessed himself of their secrets and insinuated himself into their confidences. But best of all he loved the children. When they told him their sorrows, the answering tears sprang to his eyes; when they told him of their delights, his laugh woke the echoes of the Shetucket as light and free as their own.

He laughed frequently when with the children, throwing back his great head, while the tears of mirth ran from his blue eyes. His teeth were like pearls, and constituted his chief charm. For the rest he was rugged and firmly knit. It seemed to the children, after a time, that some cloud was hanging over the serene spirit of their friend. After he had laughed he sighed, and they saw, as he walked down the green paths that led away from his place, that he would look lovingly back at the old homestead and shake his head again and again with a perplexed and melancholy air. The merchants, too, observed that he began to be closer in his bargains, and he barrelled his apples so greedily that the birds and the children were quite robbed of their autumnal feast. A winter wore away and left Micah in this changed mood. He sat through the long, dull days brooding over his fire and smoking. He made his own simple meals of mush and bacon, kept his own counsels, and neither visited nor received the neighbouring folk.

One day, in a heavy January rain, the boys noticed a strange man who rode rapidly through the village and drew rein at Micah Rood's orchard gate. He passed through the leafless orchard and up the muddy garden paths to the old dismantled house. The boys had time to learn by heart every good point of the chestnut mare fastened to the palings before the stranger emerged from the house. Micah followed him to the gate. The stranger swung himself upon the mare with a sort of jaunty flourish, while Micah stood heavily and moodily by, chewing the end of a straw.

"Well, Master Rood," the boys heard the stranger say, "thou'st till the first of next May, but not a day of grace more." He had a decisive, keen manner that took away the breath of the boys, used to men of slow action and slow speech. "Mind ye," he snapped, like an angry cur, "not another day's grace." Micah said not a word, but stolidly chewed on his straw, while the stranger cut his animal briskly with the whip, and mare and rider dashed away down the dreary road. The boys began to frisk about their old friend and pull savagely at the tails of his coat, whooping and whistling to arouse him from his reverie. Micah looked up and roared:

"Off with ye! I'm in no mood for pranks."

As a pet dog slinks away in humiliation at a blow, so the boys, hurt and indignant, skulked down the road, speechless at the cruelty of their old friend.

The April sunshine was bringing the dank odours from the earth when the village beauties were thrown into a flutter of excitement. Old Geoffry Peterkin, the peddler, came with such jewellery, such stuffs, and such laces as the maidens of Shetucket had never seen the like of before.

"You are getting rich, Geoffry," the men said to him.

"No, no!" and Geoffry shook his grizzled head with a flattered smile. "Not from you womenfolk. There's no such bargain-drivers between here and Boston town."

"Thou'lt be a setting up in Boston town, Geoffry," said another. "Thou'rt getting too fine to travel pack a-back amongst us simple country folk."

"Not a bit of it," protested Geoffry. "I couldn't let the pretty dears go without their beads and their ribbons. I come and go as reg'lar as the leaves, spring, summer, and autumn."

By twilight Geoffry had made his last visit, and with his pack somewhat lightened he tramped away in the raw dusk. He went straight down the road that led to the next village, until out of sight of the windows, then turned to his right and groped his way across the commons with his eye ever fixed on a deeper blackness in the gloom. This looming blackness was the orchard of Micah Rood. He found the gate, entered, and made his way to the dismantled house. A bat swept its wing against his face as he rapped his stick upon the door.

"What witchcraft's here?" he said, and pounded harder.

There were no cracks in the heavy oaken door through which a light might filter, and old Geoffry Peterkin was blinded like any owl when the door was flung open, and Micah Rood, with a forked candlestick in his hands, appeared, recognized him, and bade him enter. The wind drove down the hallway, blew the flame an inch from the wicks, where it burned blue a moment, and then expired, leaving the men in darkness. Geoffry stepped in, and Micah threw his weight against the door, swung the bar into place, and led Geoffry into a large bare room lit up by a blazing hickory fire. When the candles were relit, Micah said:

"Hast thou supped this night, friend Peterkin?"

"That have I not, though Rogers the smith would have made me welcome. But I waited to sup with thee, friend Rood. I like thy cakes and I like better thy company."

Micah made up the fire and swung the kettle over the blaze. He drew up a table and set dishes on it, warmed half a fowl in the pot, raked potatoes from the ashes and cut slices from the big loaf.

"I buy my bread of Hannah Stebbins, and she doth give good measure," remarked Micah, interested in his domestic labours. "Also I have from her this golden butter, and these cakes of cheese made from curds. Sit to, Peterkin, and make all that is here your own."

But though the welcome was so hearty, and though the guest seemed fain for his meat, the conversation flagged somewhat. Never had these men eaten together in such silence. Some constraint rested upon them. Each flap of the shutters startled them; each squeal of the wainscot mouse pierced their ears disagreeably. Micah forced himself to speak as the meal drew near its close.

"Thou hast prospered since thou sold milk-pans to my mother, Peterkin," said he.

"I've made a fortune with that old pack," said the peddler, pointing to the corner where it lay. "Year after year I have trudged this road, and year after year has my pack been larger and my stops longer. My stuffs, too, have changed. I carry no more milk-pans. I leave that to others. I now have jewels and cloths. Why, man! There's a fortune even now in that old pack."

He arose and unstrapped the leathern bands that bound his burden. He drew from the pack a variety of jewel-cases and handed them to Micah. "I did not show these at the village," he continued, pointing over his shoulder; "I sell those in towns."

Micah clumsily opened one or two and looked at their contents with restless eyes. There were rubies as red as a serpent's tongue; silver, carved as daintily as hoar-frost, gleaming with icy diamonds; pearls that nestled like precious eggs in fairy golden nests; turquoise gleaming from beds of enamel, and bracelets of ebony capped with topaz balls.

"These," laughed Geoffry, dangling a translucent necklace of amber, "I keep to ward off ill-luck. She will be a witch indeed that gets me to sell these. But if thou'lt marry, good Master Rood, I'll give them to thy bride."

He chuckled, gasped, and gurgled mightily; but Micah checked his exuberance by looking up fiercely.

"There'll be never a bride for me," he said. "She'd be killed here with the rats and the damp rot. It takes gold to get a woman."

"Bah!"" sneered Geoffry. "It takes youth, boy; blue eyes, a good laugh, and a strong leg. Why, if a bride can be had for gold, I've got that."

He unrolled a shimmering azure satin, and took from it two bags of soft, stout leather.

"There is where I keep my yellow boys shut up!" the old fellow cried in great glee; "and when I let them out, they'll bring me anything I want, Micah Rood, except a true heart. How have things prospered with thee?" he added, as he shot a shrewd glance at Micah from beneath his eyebrows.

"Bad," confessed Micah, "very bad. Everything has been against me of late."

"I say, boy," cried the peddler, suddenly, "I haven't been over this old house for years. Take the light and show us around."

"No," said Micah, shaking his head doggedly. "It is in bad shape, and I would feel that I was showing a friend who was in rags."

"Nonsense! "cried the peddler, bursting into a hearty laugh. "Thou need'st not fear, I'll ne'er cut thy old friend."

He had replaced his stuffs, and now seized the branched candlestick and waved his hand toward the door.

"Lead the way," he cried. "I want to see how things look;" and Micah Rood sullenly obeyed.

From room to room they went in the miserable cold and the gloom. The candle threw a faint gleam through the unkept apartments, noxious with dust and decay. Not a flaw escaped the eye of the peddler. He ran his fingers into the cracks of the doors, he counted the panes of broken glass, he remarked the gaps in the plastering.

"The dry rot has got into the wainscoting," he said jauntily.

Micah Rood was burning with impotent anger. He tried to lead the peddler past one door, but the old man's keen eyes were too quick for him, and he kicked the door open with his foot.

"What have we here?" he cried.

It was the room where Micah and his brothers had slept when they were children. The little dismantled beds stood side by side. A work-bench with some miniature tools was by the curtainless window. Everything that met his gaze brought with it a flood of early recollections.

"Here's a rare lot of old truck," Geoffry cried. "The first thing I should do would be to pitch this out of doors."

Micah caught him by the arm and pushed him from the room.

"It happens that it is not thine to pitch," he said.

Geoffry Peterkin began to laugh a low, irritating chuckle. He laughed all the way back to the room where the fire was. He laughed still as Micah showed him his room—the room where he was to pass the night; chuckled and guffawed, and clapped Micah on the back as they finally bade each other goodnight. The master of the house went back and stood before the dying fire alone.

"What did he mean in God's name?" he asked himself. "Does he know of the mortgage?"

Micah knew that the peddler who was well off frequently negotiated and dealt in the commercial paper of farmers. Pride and anger tore at his heart, like wild beasts. What would the neighbours say when they saw his father's son driven from the house that had belonged to the family for generations? How could he endure their surprise and contempt. What would the children say when they found a stranger in possession of the famous apple-trees? "I've got no more to pay it with," he cried in helpless anguish, "than I had the day the cursed lawyer came here with his threats."

He determined to find out what Peterkin knew of the matter. He spread a bear's skin before the fire and threw himself upon it and fell into a feverish sleep, which ended long before the purple dawn broke.

He cooked a breakfast of bacon and corn cake, made a cup of coffee, and aroused his guest. The peddler clean, keen, and alert, noted slyly the sullen heaviness of Micah. The meal was eaten in silence, and when it was finished, Geoffry put on his cloak, adjusted his pack, and prepared to leave. Micah put on his hat, took a pruning-knife from a shelf, remarking as he did so:

"I go early about my work in the orchard;" and followed the peddler to the door. The trees in the orchard had begun to shimmer with young green. The perfume, so familiar to Micah, so suggestive of the place that he held dearer than all the rest of the world beside, wrought upon him till his curiosity got the better of his discretion.

"It is hard work for one man to keep up a place like this and make it pay," he remarked.

Geoffry smiled slyly, but said nothing.

"Bad luck has got the start of me of late," the master continued, with an attempt at real candour.

The peddler knocked the tops off some gaunt, dead weeds that stood by the path.

"So I have heard," he said.

"What else didst thou hear?" cried Micah, quickly, his face burning, and shame and anger flashing from his blue eyes.

"Well," said the peddler, with a great show of caution, "I heard the mortgage was a good investment for anyone who wanted to buy."

"Perhaps thou know'st more about it than that," sneered Micah.

Peterkin blew on his hands and rubbed them with a knowing air.

"Well," he said, "I know what I know."

"Do you," cried Micah, clinching his fist, "out with it!"

The peddler was getting heated. He thrust his hand into his breast and drew out a paper.

"When May comes about. Master Rood, I'll ask thee to look at the face of this document."

"Thou art a sneak!" foamed Micah. "A white-livered, cowardly sneak!"

"Rough words to call a man on his own property," said the peddler, with a malicious grin.

The insult was the deepest he could have offered to the man before him. A flood of ungovernable emotions rushed over Micah. The impulse, latent in all angry animals to strike, to crush, to kill, came over him. He rushed forward madly; then the passion ebbed, and he saw the peddler on the ground. The pruning-knife in his own hand was red with blood. He gazed in cold horror; then tried in a weak, trembling way to heap leaves upon the body to hide it from his sight. He could gather only small handfuls, and they fluttered away in the wind.

The light was getting brighter. People would soon be passing down the road. He walked up and down aimlessly for a time, and then ran to the garden. He returned with a spade and began digging furiously. He made a trench between the dead man and the tree under which he had fallen; and when it was finished he pushed the body in with his foot, not daring to touch it with his hands.

Of the peddler's death there was no doubt. The rigid face and the blood-drenched garments over the heart attested the fact. So copiously had the blood gushed forth that all the soil, and the dead leaves about the body, and the exposed roots of the tree were stained with it. Involuntarily Micah looked up at the tree. He uttered an exclamation of dismay. It was the tree of the gold apples.

After a moment's silence he recommenced his work and tossed back the earth in mad haste. He smoothed it so carefully that when he had finished not even a mound appeared. He scattered dead leaves over the freshly turned ground, and then walked slowly back to the house.

For the first time the shadow that hung over it, the gloom deep as despair that looked from its vacant windows, struck him. The gloss of familiarity had hidden from his eyes what had long been patent to others—the decay, the ruin, the solitude. It swept over him as an icy breaker sweeps over a drowning man. The rats ran from him as he entered the hall. He held the arm on which the blood was rapidly drying far from him, as if he feared to let it touch his body with its confession of crime. The sleeve had stiffened to the arm, and inspired him with a nervous horror, as if a reptile was twined about it.

He flung off his coat, and finally, trembling and sick, divested himself of a flannel undergarment, but still, from finger-tip to elbow, there were blotches and smears on his arm. He realized at once the necessity of destroying the garments; and, naked to the waist, he stirred up the dying embers of the fire and threw the garments on. The heavy flannel of the coat refused to burn, and he prodded it deeper in with a poker till he saw with dismay that he had quenched the fire.

"It is fate!" he cried; "I cannot destroy them."

He lit a fire three times, but his haste and his confused horror made him throw on the heavy garments every time and strangle the infant blaze. At last he took them to the garret and locked them in an old chest. Starting at the shadows among the rafters and the creaking of the boards, he crept back through the biting chill of the vacant rooms to the one that he occupied, and washed his arm again and again, until the deep glow on it seemed like another bloodstain.

After that, for weeks he worked in his garden by day, and at night slept on the floor with the candles burning, and his hand on his flintlock.

Meanwhile in the orchard the leaves budded and spread and the perfumed blossoms came. The branches of the tree of the gold apples grew pink with swelling buds. Near that spot Micah never went; he felt as if his feet would be grasped by spectral hands.

One night a swelling wind arose, strong, steady, warm, seemingly palpable to the touch like a fabric. In the morning the orchard had flung all its banners to the air. It dazzled Micah's eyes as he looked upon the tossing clouds of pink and white fragrance. But as his eye roamed about the waving splendour he caught sight of a thing that riveted him to the spot with awe.

The tree of the gold apples had blossomed blood-red!

That day he did no work. He sat from early morning till the light waned in the west, gazing at the tree flaunting its brilliant blossoms against the sky. Few neighbours came that way; and as the tree stood in the heart of the orchard, fewer yet noticed its accursed beauty. To those that did Micah stammeringly gave a hint of some ingenious ingrafting, the secret of which was to make his fortune. But though the rest of the world wondered and wagged its head and doubted not that it was some witch-craft, the children were enraptured. They stole into the orchard and pilfered handfuls of the roseate flowers, and bore them away to school; the girls fastened them in their braids or wore them above their innocent hearts, and the boys trimmed their hat-bands and danced away in glee like youthful Corydons.

Spring-time passed and its promises of plenty were fulfilled. In the garden there grew a luxury of greenness; in the orchard the boughs lagged low. Micah Rood toiled day and night. He visited no house, he sought no company. If a neighbour saw him in the field and came for a chat, before he had reached the spot Micah had hidden himself.

"He used to be as ready for the news as the rest of us," said they to themselves, "and he had a laugh like a horse. His sweet-heart has jilted him, most like."

When the purple on the grapes began to glow through the amber, and the mellowed apples dropped from their stems, the children flocked about the orchard gate like buzzards about a battlefield. But they found the gate padlocked and the board fence pricking with pointed sticks. Micah they saw but seldom, and his face, once so sunny, was as terrible to them as the angel's with the flaming sword that kept guard over the gates of Eden. So the sinless little Adams and Eves had no choice but to turn away with empty pockets.

However, one morning, accident took Micah to the bolted gate just as the children came trooping home in the early autumn sunset; for in those days they kept students of any age at work as many hours of the day as possible. A little fay, with curls as sunny as the tendrils of the grape, caught sight of him first. Her hat was wreathed with scarlet maple leaves; her dress was as ruddy as the cheeks of the apples. She seemed a sprite of autumn. She ran toward him, with arms outstretched, crying

"Oh, Master Rood! Do come and play. Where hast thou been so long? We have wanted some apples, and the plaguy old gate was locked."

For the first time for months the pall of remembrance that hung over Micah's dead happiness was lifted, and the spirit of that time came back to him. He caught the little one in his brawny arms and threw her high, while she shrieked with terror and delight. After this the children gave no quarter. The breach begun, they sallied in and stormed the fortress. Like a dream of water to a man who is perishing of thirst, who knows while he yet dreams that he must wake and find his bliss an agony, was this hour of innocence to Micah. He ran, and leaped, and frolicked with the children in the shade of the trees till the orchard rang with their shouts, while the sky changed from daffodil to crimson, from crimson to gray, and sank into a deep autumnal twilight. Micah stuffed their little pockets with fruit, and bade them run home. But they lingered dissatisfied.

"I wish he would give us of the golden apples," they whispered among themselves. At last one plucked up courage.

"Good Master Rood, give us of the gold apples, if thou please."

Micah shook his head sternly. They entreated him with eyes and tongues. They saw a chance for a frolic. They clung to him, climbed his back, and danced about him, shouting

"The gold apples! The gold apples!"

A sudden change came over him; he marched to the tree with a look men wear when they go to battle.

"There is blood in them!" he cried hoarsely. "They are accursed—accursed!"

The children shrieked with delight at what they thought a jest.

"Blood in the apples! Ha! ha! ha!" and they rolled over one another on the grass, fighting for the windfalls.

"I tell ye 'tis so!" Micah continued. He took one of the apples and broke it into halves.

"Look," he cried; and in his eyes there came a look in which the light of reason was waning. The children pressed about him, peeping over each other at the apple. On the broken side of both halves, from the rind to the core, was a blood-red streak the width of a child's little finger. An amazed silence fell on the little group.

"Home with ye now!" he cried huskily. "Home with ye, and tell what ye have seen! Run, ye brats!"

"Then let us take some of the apples with us," they persisted.

"Ha!" he cried, "ye tale-bearers! I know the trick ye'd play! Here then—"

He shook the tree like a giant. The apples rolled to the ground so fast that they looked like strands of amber beads. The children, laughing and shouting, gathered them as they fell. They began to compare the red spots. In some the drop of blood was found just under the skin, a thin streak of carmine that penetrated to the core and coloured the silvery pulp; in others it was an isolated clot, the size of a whortleberry; and on a few a narrow crescent of crimson reached half-way around the outside of the shining rind.

Suddenly a noise, not loud but agonising, startled the little ones. They looked up at their friend. He had become horrible. His face was contorted until it was unrecognizable; his eyes were fixed on the ground as if he beheld a spectre there. Shrieking, they ran from the orchard, nor cast one fearful glance behind.

The next day the smith, filled with curiosity by the tales of the children, found an odd hour in which to visit Micah Rood's house. He invited the tailor, a man thin with hunger for gossip, to go with him. The gate of the orchard stood open, flapping on its hinges as the children had left it. The visitors sauntered through, thinking to find Micah in the house, for it was the noon hour. They tasted of this fruit and that—tried a pear, now an apricot, now a pippin,

"The tree of the gold apples is right in the centre," said the smith.

He pointed. The tailor looked; then his legs doubled under him as naturally as they ever did on the bench. The smith looked; his arm dropped by his side. After a time the two men went on, clinging to each other like children in the dark.

Micah Rood, with his sunny hair tangled in the branches, his tongue black and protruding, his face purple, and his clinched hands stained with dirt, hung from the tree of the golden apples. Beneath him, in a trench from which the ground had been clawed by human hands, was a shapeless, discoloured bundle of clothes. A skull lay at one end of the trench, and beneath it a mouldy pack was found with precious stones amid the decaying contents.

The House That Was Not

Bart Fleming took his bride out to his ranch on the plains when she was but seventeen years old, and the two set up house-keeping in three hundred and twenty acres of corn and rye. Off toward the west there was an unbroken sea of tossing corn at that time of the year when the bride came out, and as her sewing window was on the side of the house which faced the sunset, she passed a good part of each day looking into that great rustling mass, breathing in its succulent odours and listening to its sibilant melody. It was her picture gallery, her opera, her spectacle, and, being sensible,—or perhaps, being merely happy,— she made the most of it.

When harvesting time came and the corn was cut, she had much entertainment in discovering what lay beyond. The town was east, and it chanced that she had never ridden west. So, when the rolling hills of this newly beholden land lifted themselves for her contemplation, and the harvest sun, all in an angry and sanguinary glow sank in the veiled horizon, and at noon a scarf of golden vapour wavered up and down along the earth line, it was as if a new world had been made for her. Sometimes, at the coming of a storm, a whiplash of purple cloud, full of electric agility, snapped along the western horizon.

"Oh, you'll see a lot of queer things on these here plains," her husband said when she spoke to him of these phenomena. "I guess what you see is the wind."

"The wind!" cried Flora. "You can't see the wind, Bart."

"Now look here, Flora," returned Bart, with benevolent emphasis, "you're a smart one, but you don't know all I know about this here country. I've lived here three mortal years, waitin' for you to git up out of your mother's arms and come out to keep me company, and I know what there is to know. Some things out here is queer—so queer folks wouldn't believe 'em unless they saw. An' some's so pig-headed they don't believe their own eyes. As for th' wind, if you lay down flat and squint toward th' west, you can see it blowin' along near th' ground, like a big ribbon; an' sometimes it's th' colour of air, an' sometimes it's silver an' gold, an' sometimes, when a storm is comin', it's purple."

"If you got so tired looking at the wind, why didn't you marry some other girl, Bart, instead of waiting for me?"

Flora was more interested in the first part of Bart's speech than in the last.

"Oh, come on!" protested Bart, and he picked her up in his arms and jumped her toward the ceiling of the low shack as if she were a little girl—but then, to be sure, she wasn't much more.

Of all the things Flora saw when the corn was cut down, nothing interested her so much as a low cottage, something like her own, which lay away in the distance. She could not guess how far it might be, because distances are deceiving out there, where the altitude is high and the air is as clear as one of those mystic balls of glass in which the sallow mystics of India see the moving shadows of the future.

She had not known there were neighbours so near, and she wondered for several days about them before she ventured to say anything to Bart on the subject. Indeed, for some reason which she did not attempt to explain to herself, she felt shy about broaching the matter. Perhaps Bart did not want her to know the people. The thought came to her, as naughty thoughts will come, even to the best of persons, that some handsome young men might be "baching" it out there by themselves, and Bart didn't wish her to make their acquaintance. Bart had flattered her so much that she had actually begun to think herself beautiful, though as a matter of fact she was only a nice little girl with a lot of reddish-brown hair, and a bright pair of reddish-brown eyes in a white face.

"Bart," she ventured one evening, as the sun, at its fiercest, rushed toward the great black hollow of the west, "who lives over there in that shack?"

She turned away from the window where she had been looking at the incarnadined disk, and she thought she saw Bart turn pale. But then, her eyes were so blurred with the glory she had been gazing at, that she might easily have been mistaken.

"I say, Bart, why don't you speak? If there's anyone around to associate with, I should think you'd let me have the benefit of their company. It isn't as funny as you think, staying here alone days and days."

"You ain't gettin' homesick, be you, sweetheart?" cried Bart, putting his arms around her. "You ain't gettin' tired of my society, be yeh?"

It took some time to answer this question in a satisfactory manner, but at length Flora was able to return to her original topic.

"But the shack, Bart! Who lives there, anyway?"

"I'm not acquainted with 'em," said Bart, sharply. "Ain't them biscuits done, Flora?"

Then, of course, she grew obstinate.

"Those biscuits will never be done, Bart, till I know about that house, and why you never spoke of it, and why nobody ever comes down the road from there. Someone lives there I know, for in the mornings and at night I see the smoke coming out of the chimney."

"Do you now?" cried Bart, opening his eyes and looking at her with unfeigned interest. "Well, do you know, sometimes I've fancied I seen that too?"

"Well, why not," cried Flora, in half anger. "Why shouldn't you?"

"See here, Flora, take them biscuits out an' listen to me. There ain't no house there. Hello! I didn't know you'd go for to drop the biscuits. Wait, I'll help you pick 'em up. By cracky, they're hot, ain't they? What you puttin' a towel over 'em for? Well, you set down here on my knee, so. Now you look over at that there house. You see it, don't yeh? Well, it ain't there! No! I saw it the first week I was out here. I was jus' half dyin', thinkin' of you an' wonderin' why you didn't write. That was the time you was mad at me. So I rode over there one day—lookin' up company, so t' speak—and there wa'n't no house there. I spent all one Sunday lookin' for it. Then I spoke to Jim Geary about it. He laughed an' got a little white about th' gills, an' he said he guessed I'd have to look a good while before I found it. He said that there shack was an ole joke."

"Why—what—"

"Well, this here is th' story he tol' me. He said a man an' his wife come out here t' live an' put up that there little place. An' she was young, you know, an' kind o' skeery, and she got lonesome. It worked on her an' worked on her, an' one day she up an' killed the baby an' her husband an' herself. Th' folks found 'em and buried 'em right there on their own ground. Well, about two weeks after that, th' house was burned down. Don't know how. Tramps, maybe. Anyhow, it burned. At least, I guess it burned!"

"You guess it burned!"

"Well, it ain't there, you know."

"But if it burned the ashes are there."

"All right, girlie, they're there then. Now let's have tea."

This they proceeded to do, and were happy and cheerful all evening, but that didn't keep Flora from rising at the first flush of dawn and stealing out of the house. She looked away over west as she went to the barn and there, dark and firm against the horizon, stood the little house against the pellucid sky of morning. She got on Ginger's back—Ginger being her own yellow broncho—and set off at a hard pace for the house. It didn't appear to come any nearer, but the objects which had seemed to be beside it came closer into view, and Flora pressed on, with her mind steeled for anything. But as she approached the poplar windbreak which stood to the north of the house, the little shack waned like a shadow before her. It faded and dimmed before her eyes.

She slapped Ginger's flanks and kept him going, and she at last got him up to the spot. But there was nothing there. The bunch grass grew tall and rank and in the midst of it lay a baby's shoe. Flora thought of picking it up, but something cold in her veins withheld her. Then she grew angry, and set Ginger's head toward the place and tried to drive him over it. But the yellow broncho gave one snort of fear, gathered himself in a bunch, and then, all tense, leaping muscles, made for home as only a broncho can.

The Piano Next Door

Babette had gone away for the summer; the furniture was in its summer linens; the curtains were down, and Babette's husband, John Boyce, was alone in the house. It was the first year of his marriage, and he missed Babette. But then, as he often said to himself, he ought never to have married her. He did it from pure selfishness, and because he was determined to possess the most illusive, tantalizing, elegant, and utterly unmoral little creature that the sun shone upon. He wanted her because she reminded him of birds, and flowers, and summer winds, and other exquisite things created for the delectation of mankind. He neither expected nor desired her to think. He had half-frightened her into marrying him, had taken her to a poor man's home, provided her with no society such as she had been accustomed to, and he had no reasonable cause of complaint when she answered the call of summer and flitted away, like a butterfly in the morning sunshine, to the place where the flowers grew.

He wrote to her every evening, sitting in the stifling, ugly house, and poured out his soul as if it were a libation to a goddess. She sometimes answered by telegraph, sometimes by a perfumed note. He schooled himself not to feel hurt. Why should Babette write? Does a goldfinch indict epistles; or a hummingbird study composition; or a glancing, red-scaled fish in summer shallows consider the meaning of words?

He knew at the beginning what Babette was—guessed her limitations—trembled when he buttoned her tiny glove—kissed her dainty slipper when he found it in the closet after she was gone—thrilled at the sound of her laugh, or the memory of it! That was all. A mere case of love. He was in bonds. Babette was not. Therefore he was in the city, working overhours to pay for Babette's pretty follies down at the seaside. It was quite right and proper. He was a grub in the furrow; she a lark in the blue. Those had always been and always must be their relative positions.

Having attained a mood of philosophic calm, in which he was prepared to spend his evenings alone—as became a grub— and to await with dignified patience the return of his wife, it was in the nature of an inconsistency that he should have walked the floor of the dull little drawing-room like a lion in cage. It did not seem in keeping with the position of superior serenity which he had assumed, that, reading Babette's notes, he should have raged with jealousy, or that, in the loneliness of his unkempt chamber, he should have stretched out arms of longing. Even if Babette had been present, she would only have smiled her gay little smile and coquetted with him. She could not understand. He had known, of course, from the first moment, that she could not understand! And so, why the ache, ache, ache of the heart! Or *was* it the heart, or the brain, or the soul?

Sometimes, when the evenings were so hot that he could not endure the close air of the house, he sat on the narrow, dusty front porch and looked about him at his neighbours. The street had once been smart and aspiring, but it had fallen into decay and dejection. Pale young men, with flurried-looking wives, seemed to Boyce to occupy most of the houses. Some- times three or four couples would live in one house. Most of these appeared to be childless. The women made a pretence at fashionable dressing, and wore their hair elaborately in fashions which somehow suggested boarding-houses to Boyce, though he could not have told why.

Every house in the block needed fresh paint. Lacking this renovation, the householders tried to make up for it by a display of lace curtains which, at every window, swayed in the smoke- weighted breeze. Strips of carpeting were laid down the front steps of the houses where the communities of young couples

126

lived, and here, evenings, the inmates of the houses gathered, committing mild extravagances such as the treating of each other to ginger ale, or beer, or ice-cream.

Boyce watched these tawdry makeshifts at sociability with bitterness and loathing. He wondered how he could have been such a fool as to bring his exquisite Babette to this neighbourhood. How could he expect that she would return to him? It was not reasonable. He ought to go down on his knees with gratitude that she even condescended to write him.

Sitting one night till late,—so late that the fashionable young wives with their husbands had retired from the strips of stair carpeting,—and raging at the loneliness which ate at his heart like a cancer, he heard, softly creeping through the windows of the house adjoining his own, the sound of comfortable melody.

It breathed upon his ear like a spirit of consolation, speaking of peace, of love which needs no reward save its own sweetness, of aspiration which looks forever beyond the thing of the hour to find attainment in that which is eternal. So insidiously did it whisper these things, so delicately did the simple and perfect melodies creep upon the spirit—that Boyce felt no resentment, but from the first listened as one who listens to learn, or as one who, fainting on the hot road, hears, far in the ferny deeps below, the gurgle of a spring.

Then came harmonies more intricate: fair fabrics of woven sound, in the midst of which gleamed golden threads of joy; a tapestry of sound, multi-tinted, gallant with story and achievement, and beautiful things. Boyce, sitting on his absurd *piazza*, with his knees jammed against the balustrade, and his chair back against the dun-coloured wall of his house, seemed to be walking in the cathedral of the redwood forest, with blue above him, a vast hymn in his ears, pungent perfume in his nostrils, and mighty shafts of trees lifting themselves to heaven, proud and erect as pure men before their Judge. He stood on a mountain at sunrise, and saw the marvels of the amethystine clouds below his feet, heard an eternal and white silence, such as broods among the everlasting snows, and saw an eagle winging for the sun.

127

He was in a city, and away from him, diverging like the spokes of a wheel, ran thronging streets, and to his sense came the beat, beat, beat of the city's heart. He saw the golden alchemy of a chosen race; saw greed transmitted to progress; saw that which had enslaved men, work at last to their liberation; heard the roar of mighty mills, and on the streets all the peoples of earth walking with common purpose, in fealty and understanding. And then, from the swelling of this concourse of great sounds, came a diminuendo, calm as philosophy, and from that, nothingness.

Boyce sat still for a long time, listening to the echoes which this music had awakened in his soul. He retired, at length, content, but determined that upon the morrow he would watch—the day being Sunday—for the musician who had so moved and taught him.

He arose early, therefore, and having prepared his own simple breakfast of fruit and coffee, took his station by the window to watch for the man. For he felt convinced that the exposition he had heard was that of a masculine mind. The long, hot hours of the morning went by, but the front door of the house next to his did not open.

"These artists sleep late," he complained. Still he watched. He was too much afraid of losing him to go out for dinner. By three in the afternoon he had grown impatient. He went to the house next door and rang the bell. There was no response. He thundered another appeal. An old woman with a cloth about her head answered the door. She was very deaf, and Boyce had difficulty in making himself understood.

"The family is in the country," was all she would say. "The family will not be home till September."

"But there is some one living here?" shouted Boyce.

"*I* live here," she said with dignity, putting back a wisp of dirty gray hair behind her ear. "It is my house. I sublet to the family."

"What family?"

But the old creature was not communicative.

"The family that lives here," she said.

"Then who plays the piano in this house?" roared Boyce. "Do you?"

He thought a shade of pallor showed itself on her ash-coloured cheeks. Yet she smiled a little at the idea of her playing.

"There is no piano," she said, and she put an enigmatical emphasis to the words.

"Nonsense," cried Boyce, indignantly. "I heard a piano being played in this very house for hours last night!"

"You may enter," said the old woman, with an accent more vicious than hospitable.

Boyce almost burst into the drawing-room. It was a dusty and forbidding place, with ugly furniture and gaudy walls. No piano nor any other musical instrument stood in it. The intruder turned an angry and baffled face to the old woman, who was smiling with ill-concealed exultation.

"I shall see the other rooms," he announced. The old woman did not appear to be surprised at his impertinence.

"As you please," she said.

So, with the hobbling creature, with her bandaged head, for a guide, he explored every room of the house, which being identical with his own, he could do without fear of leaving any apartment unentered. But no piano did he find!

"Explain," roared Boyce at length, turning upon the leering old hag beside him. "Explain! For surely I heard music more beautiful than I can tell."

"I know nothing," she said. "But it is true I once had a lodger who rented the front room, and that he played upon the piano. I am poor at hearing, but he must have played well, for all the neighbors used to come in front of the house to listen, and sometimes they applauded him, and sometimes they were still. I could tell by watching their hands. Sometimes little children came and danced. Other times young men and women came and listened. But the young man died. The neighbours were angry. They came to look at him and said he had starved to death. It was no fault of mine. I sold his piano to pay his funeral expenses—and it took every cent to pay for them too, I'd have you know. But since then, sometimes—still, it must be nonsense, for I never heard it—folks say that he plays the piano in my room. It has kept me out of the letting of it more than once. But the family doesn't seem to mind—the family that lives here, you know. They will be back in September. Yes."

Boyce left her nodding her thanks at what he had placed in her hand, and went home to write it all to Babette—Babette who would laugh so merrily when she read it!

The Room of the Evil Thought

They called it the room of the Evil Thought. It was really the pleasantest room in the house, and when the place had been used as the rectory, was the minister's study. It looked out on a mournful clump of larches, such as may often be seen in the old-fashioned yards in Michigan, and these threw a tender gloom over the apartment.

There was a wide fireplace in the room, and it had been the young minister's habit to sit there hours and hours, staring ahead of him at the fire, and smoking moodily. The replenishing of the fire and of his pipe, it was said, would afford him occupation all the day long, and that was how it came about that his parochial duties were neglected so that, little by little, the people became dissatisfied with him, though he was an eloquent young man, who could send his congregation away drunk on his influence. However, the calmer pulsed among his parish began to whisper that it was indeed the influence of the young minister and not that of the Holy Ghost which they felt, and it was finally decided that neither animal magnetism nor hypnotism were good substitutes for religion. And so they let him go.

The new rector moved into a smart brick house on the other side of the church, and gave receptions and dinner parties, and was punctilious about making his calls. The people therefore liked him very much—so much that they raised the debt on the church and bought a chime of bells, in their enthusiasm. Every one was lighter of heart than under the ministration of the previous rector. A burden appeared to be lifted from the community. True, there were a few who confessed the new man did not give them the food for thought which the old one had done, but, then, the former rector had made them uncomfortable! He had not only made them conscious of the sins of which they were already guilty, but also of those for which they had the latent capacity. A strange and fatal man, whom women loved to their sorrow, and whom simple men could not understand! It was generally agreed that the parish was well rid of him.

"He was a genius," said the people in commiseration. The word was an uncomplimentary epithet with them.

When the Hanscoms moved in the house which had been the old rectory, they gave Grandma Hanscom the room with the fireplace. Grandma was well pleased. The roaring fire warmed her heart as well as her chill old body, and she wept with weak joy when she looked at the larches, because they reminded her of the house she had lived in when she was first married. All the forenoon of the first day she was busy putting things away in bureau drawers and closets, but by afternoon she was ready to sit down in her high-backed rocker and enjoy the comforts of her room.

She nodded a bit before the fire, as she usually did after luncheon, and then she awoke with an awful start and sat staring before her with such a look in her gentle, filmy old eyes as had never been there before. She did not move, except to rock slightly, and the Thought grew and grew till her face was disguised as by some hideous mask of tragedy.

By and by the children came pounding at the door.

"Oh, grandma, let us in, please. We want to see your new room, and mamma gave us some ginger cookies on a plate, and we want to give some to you."

The door gave way under their assaults, and the three little ones stood peeping in, waiting for permission to enter. But it did not seem to be their grandma—their own dear grandma—who arose and tottered toward them in fierce haste, crying:

"Away, away! Out of my sight! Out of my sight before I do the thing I want to do! Such a terrible thing! Send someone to me quick, children, children! Send someone quick!"

They fled with feet shod with fear, and their mother came, and Grandma Hanscom sank down and clung about her skirts and sobbed:

"Tie me, Miranda. Make me fast to the bed or the wall. Get someone to watch me. For I want to do an awful thing!"

They put the trembling old creature in bed, and she raved there all the night long and cried out to be held, and to be kept from doing the fearful thing, whatever it was—for she never said what it was.

The next morning someone suggested taking her in the sitting-room where she would be with the family. So they laid her on the sofa, hemmed around with cushions, and before long she was her quiet self again, though exhausted, naturally, with the tumult of the previous night. Now and then, as the children played about her, a shadow crept over her face—a shadow as of cold remembrance—and then the perplexed tears followed.

When she seemed as well as ever they put her back in her room. But though the fire glowed and the lamp burned, as soon as ever she was alone they heard her shrill cries ringing to them that the Evil Thought had come again. So Hal, who was home from college, carried her up to his room, which she seemed to like very well. Then he went down to have a smoke before grandma's fire.

The next morning he was absent from breakfast. They thought he might have gone for an early walk, and waited for him a few minutes. Then his sister went to the room that looked upon the larches, and found him dressed and pacing the floor with a face set and stern. He had not been in bed at all, as she saw at once. His eyes were bloodshot, his face stricken as if with old age or sin or—but she could not make it out. When he saw her he sank in a chair and covered his face with his hands, and between the trembling fingers she could see drops of perspiration on his forehead.

"Hal!" she cried, "Hal, what is it?"

But for answer he threw his arms about the little table and

clung to it, and looked at her with tortured eyes, in which she fancied she saw a gleam of hate. She ran, screaming, from the room, and her father came and went up to him and laid his hands on the boy's shoulders. And then a fearful thing happened. All the family saw it. There could be no mistake. Hal's hands found their way with frantic eagerness toward his father's throat as if they would choke him, and the look in his eyes was so like a madman's that his father raised his fist and felled him as he used to fell men years before in the college fights, and then dragged him into the sitting-room and wept over him.

By evening, however, Hal was all right, and the family said it must have been a fever,—perhaps from overstudy,—at which Hal covertly smiled. But his father was still too anxious about him to let him out of his sight, so he put him on a cot in his room, and thus it chanced that the mother and Grace concluded to sleep together downstairs.

The two women made a sort of festival of it, and drank little cups of chocolate before the fire, and undid and brushed their brown braids, and smiled at each other, understandingly, with that sweet intuitive sympathy which women have, and Grace told her mother a number of things which she had been waiting for just such an auspicious occasion to confide.

But the larches were noisy and cried out with wild voices, and the flame of the fire grew blue and swirled about in the draught sinuously, so that a chill crept upon the two. Something cold appeared to envelop them—such a chill as pleasure voyagers feel when a berg steals beyond Newfoundland and glows blue and threatening upon their ocean path.

Then came something else which was not cold, but hot as the flames of hell—and they saw red, and stared at each other with maddened eyes, and then ran together from the room and clasped in close embrace safe beyond the fatal place, and thanked God they had not done the thing that they dared not speak of— the thing which suddenly came to them to do.

So they called it the room of the Evil Thought. They could not account for it. They avoided the thought of it, being healthy and happy folk. But none entered it more. The door was locked.

One day, Hal, reading the paper, came across a paragraph concerning the young minister who had once lived there, and who had thought and written there and so influenced the lives of those about him that they remembered him even while they disapproved.

"He cut a man's throat on board ship for Australia," said he, "and then he cut his own, without fatal effect—and jumped overboard, and so ended it. What a strange thing!"

Then they all looked at one another with subtle looks, and a shadow fell upon them and stayed the blood at their hearts.

The next week the room of the Evil Thought was pulled down to make way for a pansy bed, which is quite gay and innocent, and blooms all the better because the larches, with their eternal murmuring, have been laid low and carted away to the sawmill.

The Shape of Fear

Tim O'Connor—who was descended from the O'Conors with one N—— started life as a poet and an enthusiast. His mother had designed him for the priesthood, and at the age of fifteen, most of his verses had an ecclesiastical tinge, but, somehow or other, he got into the newspaper business instead, and became a pessimistic gentleman, with a literary style of great beauty and an income of modest proportions. He fell in with men who talked of art for art's sake,—though what right they had to speak of art at all nobody knew,—and little by little his view of life and love became more or less profane.

He met a woman who sucked his heart's blood, and he knew it and made no protest; nay, to the great amusement of the fellows who talked of art for art's sake, he went the length of marrying her. He could not in decency explain that he had the traditions of fine gentlemen behind him and so had to do as he did, because his friends might not have understood. He laughed at the days when he had thought of the priesthood, blushed when he ran across any of those tender and exquisite old verses he had written in his youth, and became addicted to absinthe and other less peculiar drinks, and to gaming a little to escape a madness of *ennui*.

As the years went by he avoided, with more and more scorn, that part of the world which he denominated Philistine, and consorted only with the fellows who flocked about Jim O'Malley's saloon. He was pleased with solitude, or with these convivial wits, and with not very much else beside. Jim O'Malley was a sort of Irish poem, set to inspiring measure. He was, in fact, a Hibernian Mæcenas, who knew better than to put bad whiskey before a man of talent, or tell a trite tale in the presence of a wit. The recountal of his disquisitions on politics and other current matters had enabled no less than three men to acquire national reputations; and a number of wretches, having gone the way of men who talk of art for art's sake, and dying in foreign lands, or hospitals, or asylums, having no one else to be homesick for, had been homesick for Jim O'Malley, and wept for the sound of his voice and the grasp of his hearty hand.

When Tim O'Connor turned his back upon most of the things he was born to and took up with the life which he consistently lived till the unspeakable end, he was unable to get rid of certain peculiarities. For example, in spite of all his debauchery, he continued to look like the Beloved Apostle. Notwithstanding abject friendships he wrote limpid and noble English. Purity seemed to dog his heels, no matter how violently he attempted to escape from her. He was never so drunk that he was not an exquisite, and even his creditors, who had become inured to his deceptions, confessed it was a privilege to meet so perfect a gentleman.

The creature who held him in bondage, body and soul, actually came to love him for his gentleness, and for some quality which baffled her, and made her ache with a strange longing which she could not define. Not that she ever defined anything, poor little beast! She had skin the color of pale gold, and yellow eyes with brown lights in them, and great plaits of straw-colored hair. About her lips was a fatal and sensuous smile, which, when it got hold of a man's imagination, would not let it go, but held to it, and mocked it till the day of his death. She was the incarnation of the Eternal Feminine, with all the wifeliness and the maternity left out—she was ancient, yet ever young, and familiar as joy or tears or sin.

She took good care of Tim in some ways: fed him well, nursed him back to reason after a period of hard drinking, saw that he put on overshoes when the walks were wet, and looked after his money. She even prized his brain, for she discovered that it was a delicate little machine which produced gold. By association with him and his friends, she learned that a number of apparently useless things had value in the eyes of certain convenient fools, and so she treasured the autographs of distinguished persons who wrote to him—autographs which he disdainfully tossed in the waste basket. She was careful with presentation copies from authors, and she went the length of urging Tim to write a book himself. But at that he balked.

"Write a book!" he cried to her, his gentle face suddenly white with passion. "Who am I to commit such a profanation?"

She didn't know what he meant, but she had a theory that it was dangerous to excite him, and so she sat up till midnight to cook a chop for him when he came home that night.

He preferred to have her sitting up for him, and he wanted every electric light in their apartments turned to the full. If, by any chance, they returned together to a dark house, he would not enter till she touched the button in the hall, and illuminated the room. Or if it so happened that the lights were turned off in the night time, and he awoke to find himself in darkness, he shrieked till the woman came running to his relief, and, with derisive laughter, turned them on again. But when she found that after these frights he lay trembling and white in his bed, she began to be alarmed for the clever, gold-making little machine, and to renew her assiduities, and to horde more tenaciously than ever, those valuable curios on which she some day expected to realize when he was out of the way, and no longer in a position to object to their barter.

O'Connor's idiosyncrasy of fear was a source of much amusement among the boys at the office where he worked. They made open sport of it, and yet, recognizing him for a sensitive plant, and granting that genius was entitled to whimsicalities, it was their custom when they called for him after work hours, to permit him to reach the lighted corridor before they turned out the gas over his desk. This, they reasoned, was but a slight service to perform for the most enchanting beggar in the world.

"Dear fellow," said Rick Dodson, who loved him, "is it the Devil you expect to see? And if so, why are you averse? Surely the Devil is not such a bad old chap."

"You haven't found him so?"

"Tim, by heaven, you know, you ought to explain to me. A citizen of the world and a student of its purlieus, like myself, ought to know what there is to know! Now you're a man of sense, in spite of a few bad habits—such as myself, for example. Is this fad of yours madness?—which would be quite to your credit,—for gadzooks, I like a lunatic! Or is it the complaint of a man who has gathered too much data on the subject of Old Rye? Or is it, as I suspect, something more occult, and therefore more interesting?"

"Rick, boy," said Tim, "you're too—inquiring!" And he turned to his desk with a look of delicate hauteur.

It was the very next night that these two tippling pessimists spent together talking about certain disgruntled but immortal gentlemen, who, having said their say and made the world quite uncomfortable, had now journeyed on to inquire into the nothingness which they postulated. The dawn was breaking in the muggy east; the bottles were empty, the cigars burnt out. Tim turned toward his friend with a sharp breaking of sociable silence.

"Rick," he said, "do you know that Fear has a Shape?"

"And so has my nose!"

"You asked me the other night what I feared. Holy father, I make my confession to you. What I fear is Fear."

"That's because you've drunk too much—or not enough.

Come, fill the cup, and in the fire of Spring

Your winter garment of repentance fling—

"My costume then would be too nebulous for this weather, dear boy. But it's true what I was saying. I am afraid of ghosts."

"For an agnostic that seems a bit—"

"Agnostic! Yes, so completely an agnostic that I do not even know that I do not know! God, man, do you mean you have no ghosts—no—no things which shape themselves? Why, there are things I have done—"

"Don't think of them, my boy! See, '*night's candles are burnt out, and jocund day stands tiptoe on the misty mountain top.*'"

Tim looked about him with a sickly smile. He looked behind him and there was nothing there; stared at the blank window, where the smoky dawn showed its offensive face, and there was nothing there. He pushed away the moist hair from his haggard face—that face which would look like the blessed St. John, and leaned heavily back in his chair.

"'*Yon light is not daylight, I know it, I,*'" he murmured drowsily, "'*it is some meteor which the sun exhales, to be to thee this night—*'"

The words floated off in languid nothingness, and he slept. Dodson arose preparatory to stretching himself on his couch. But first he bent over his friend with a sense of tragic appreciation.

"Damned by the skin of his teeth!" he muttered. "A little more, and he would have gone right, and the Devil would have lost a good fellow. As it is"—he smiled with his usual conceited delight in his own sayings, even when they were uttered in soliloquy—"he is merely one of those splendid gentlemen one will meet with in hell." Then Dodson had a momentary nostalgia for goodness himself, but he soon overcame it, and stretching himself on his sofa, he, too, slept.

That night he and O'Connor went together to hear "Faust" sung, and returning to the office, Dodson prepared to write his criticism. Except for the distant clatter of telegraph instruments, or the peremptory cries of "copy" from an upper room, the office was still. Dodson wrote and smoked his interminable cigarettes; O'Connor rested his head in his hands on the desk, and sat in perfect silence. He did not know when Dodson finished, or when, arising, and absent-mindedly extinguishing the lights, he moved to the door with his copy in his hands. Dodson gathered up the hats and coats as he passed them where they lay on a chair, and called:

"It is done, Tim. Come, let's get out of this."

There was no answer, and he thought Tim was following, but after he had handed his criticism to the city editor, he saw he was still alone, and returned to the room for his friend. He advanced no further than the doorway, for, as he stood in the dusky corridor and looked within the darkened room, he saw before his friend a Shape, white, of perfect loveliness, divinely delicate and pure and ethereal, which seemed as the embodiment of all goodness. From it came a soft radiance and a perfume softer than the wind when "*it breathes upon a bank of violets stealing and giving odour.*" Staring at it, with eyes immovable, sat his friend.

It was strange that at sight of a thing so unspeakably fair, a coldness like that which comes from the jewel-blue lips of a Muir crevasse should have fallen upon Dodson, or that it was only by summoning all the manhood that was left in him, that he was able to restore light to the room, and to rush to his friend. When he reached poor Tim he was stone-still with paralysis. They took him home to the woman, who nursed him out of that attack—and later on worried him into another.

When he was able to sit up and jeer at things a little again, and help himself to the quail the woman broiled for him, Dodson, sitting beside him, said:

"Did you call that little exhibition of yours legerdemain, Tim, you sweep? Or are you really the Devil's bairn?"

"It was the Shape of Fear," said Tim, quite seriously.

"But it seemed mild as mother's milk."

"It was compounded of the good I might have done. It is that which I fear."

He would explain no more. Later—many months later—he died patiently and sweetly in the madhouse, praying for rest. The little beast with the yellow eyes had high mass celebrated for him, which, all things considered, was almost as pathetic as it was amusing.

Dodson was in Vienna when he heard of it.

"Sa, sa!" cried he. "I wish it wasn't so dark in the tomb! What do you suppose Tim is looking at?"

As for Jim O'Malley, he was with difficulty kept from illuminating the grave with electricity.

Their Dear Little Ghost

The first time one looked at Elsbeth, one was not prepossessed. She was thin and brown, her nose turned slightly upward, her toes went in just a perceptible degree, and her hair was perfectly straight. But when one looked longer, one perceived that she was a charming little creature. The straight hair was as fine as silk, and hung in funny little braids down her back; there was not a flaw in her soft brown skin, and her mouth was tender and shapely. But her particular charm lay in a look which she habitually had, of seeming to know curious things—such as it is not allotted to ordinary persons to know. One felt tempted to say to her:

"What are these beautiful things which you know, and of which others are ignorant? What is it you see with those wise and pellucid eyes? Why is it that everybody loves you?"

Elsbeth was my little godchild, and I knew her better than I knew any other child in the world. But still I could not truthfully say that I was familiar with her, for to me her spirit was like a fair and fragrant road in the midst of which I might walk in peace and joy, but where I was continually to discover something new. The last time I saw her quite well and strong was over in the woods where she had gone with her two little brothers and her nurse to pass the hottest weeks of summer. I followed her, foolish old creature that I was, just to be near her, for I needed to dwell where the sweet aroma of her life could reach me.

One morning when I came from my room, limping a little, because I am not so young as I used to be, and the lake wind works havoc with me, my little godchild came dancing to me singing:

"Come with me and I'll show you my places, my places, my places!"

Miriam, when she chanted by the Red Sea might have been more exultant, but she could not have been more bewitching. Of course I knew what "places" were, because I had once been a little girl myself, but unless you are acquainted with the real meaning of "places," it would be useless to try to explain. Either you know "places" or you do not—just as you understand the meaning of poetry or you do not. There are things in the world which cannot be taught.

Elsbeth's two tiny brothers were present, and I took one by each hand and followed her. No sooner had we got out of doors in the woods than a sort of mystery fell upon the world and upon us. We were cautioned to move silently, and we did so, avoiding the crunching of dry twigs.

"The fairies hate noise," whispered my little godchild, her eyes narrowing like a cat's.

"I must get my wand first thing I do," she said in an awed undertone. "It is useless to try to do anything without a wand."

The tiny boys were profoundly impressed, and, indeed, so was I. I felt that at last, I should, if I behaved properly, see the fairies, which had hitherto avoided my materialistic gaze. It was an enchanting moment, for there appeared, just then, to be nothing commonplace about life.

There was a swale near by, and into this the little girl plunged. I could see her red straw hat bobbing about among the tall rushes, and I wondered if there were snakes.

"Do you think there are snakes?" I asked one of the tiny boys.

"If there are," he said with conviction, "they won't dare hurt her."

He convinced me. I feared no more. Presently Elsbeth came out of the swale. In her hand was a brown "cattail," perfectly full and round. She carried it as queens carry their sceptres—the beautiful queens we dream of in our youth.

"Come," she commanded, and waved the sceptre in a fine manner. So we followed, each tiny boy gripping my hand tight. We were all three a trifle awed. Elsbeth led us into a dark underbrush. The branches, as they flew back in our faces, left them wet with dew. A wee path, made by the girl's dear feet, guided our footsteps. Perfumes of elderberry and wild cucumber scented the air. A bird, frightened from its nest, made frantic cries above our heads. The underbrush thickened. Presently the gloom of the hemlocks was over us, and in the midst of the shadowy green a tulip tree flaunted its leaves. Waves boomed and broke upon the shore below. There was a growing dampness as we went on, treading very lightly. A little green snake ran coquettishly from us. A fat and glossy squirrel chattered at us from a safe height, stroking his whiskers with a complaisant air.

At length we reached the "place." It was a circle of velvet grass, bright as the first blades of spring, delicate as fine sea-ferns. The sunlight, falling down the shaft between the hemlocks, flooded it with a softened light and made the forest round about look like deep purple velvet. My little godchild stood in the midst and raised her wand impressively.

"This is my place," she said, with a sort of wonderful gladness in her tone. "This is where I come to the fairy balls. Do you see them?"

"See what?" whispered one tiny boy.

"The fairies."

There was a silence. The older boy pulled at my skirt.

"Do *you* see them?" he asked, his voice trembling with expectancy.

"Indeed," I said, "I fear I am too old and wicked to see fairies, and yet—are their hats red?"

"They are," laughed my little girl. "Their hats are red, and as small—as small!" She held up the pearly nail of her wee finger to give us the correct idea.

"And their shoes are very pointed at the toes?"

"Oh, very pointed!"

"And their garments are green?"

"As green as grass."

"And they blow little horns?"

"The sweetest little horns!"

"I think I see them," I cried.

"We think we see them too," said the tiny boys, laughing in perfect glee.

"And you hear their horns, don't you?" my little godchild asked somewhat anxiously.

"Don't we hear their horns?" I asked the tiny boys.

"We think we hear their horns," they cried. "Don't you think we do?"

"It must be we do," I said. "Aren't we very, very happy?"

We all laughed softly. Then we kissed each other and Elsbeth led us out, her wand high in the air.

And so my feet found the lost path to Arcady.

The next day I was called to the Pacific coast, and duty kept me there till well into December. A few days before the date set for my return to my home, a letter came from Elsbeth's mother.

"Our little girl is gone into the Unknown, that Unknown in which she seemed to be forever trying to pry. We knew she was going, and we told her. She was quite brave, but she begged us to try some way to keep her till after Christmas. 'My presents are not finished yet,' she made moan. 'And I did so want to see what I was going to have. You can't have a very happy Christmas without me, I should think. Can you arrange to keep me somehow till after then?' We could not 'arrange' either with God in heaven or science upon earth, and she is gone."

She was only my little godchild, and I am an old maid, with no business fretting over children, but it seemed as if the medium of light and beauty had been taken from me. Through this crystal soul I had perceived whatever was loveliest. However, what was, was! I returned to my home and took up a course of Egyptian history, and determined to concern myself with nothing this side the Ptolemies.

Her mother has told me how, on Christmas eve, as usual, she and Elsbeth's father filled the stockings of the little ones, and hung them, where they had always hung, by the fireplace. They had little heart for the task, but they had been prodigal that year in their expenditures, and had heaped upon the two tiny boys all the treasures they thought would appeal to them. They asked themselves how they could have been so insane previously as to exercise economy at Christmas time, and what they meant by not getting Elsbeth the autoharp she had asked for the year before.

"And now—" began her father, thinking of harps. But he could not complete this sentence, of course, and the two went on passionately and almost angrily with their task. There were two stockings and two piles of toys. Two stockings only, and only two piles of toys! Two is very little!

They went away and left the darkened room, and after a time they slept—after a long time. Perhaps that was about the time the tiny boys awoke, and, putting on their little dressing gowns and bed slippers, made a dash for the room where the Christmas things were always placed. The older one carried a candle which gave out a feeble light. The other followed behind through the silent house. They were very impatient and eager, but when they reached the door of the sitting-room they stopped, for they saw that another child was before them.

It was a delicate little creature, sitting in her white night gown, with two rumpled funny braids falling down her back, and she seemed to be weeping. As they watched, she arose, and putting out one slender finger as a child does when she counts, she made sure over and over again—three sad times—that there were only two stockings and two piles of toys! Only those and no more.

The little figure looked so familiar that the boys started toward it, but just then, putting up her arm and bowing her face in it, as Elsbeth had been used to do when she wept or was offended, the little thing glided away and went out. That's what the boys said. It went out as a candle goes out.

They ran and woke their parents with the tale, and all the house was searched in a wonderment, and disbelief, and hope, and tumult! But nothing was found. For nights they watched. But there was only the silent house. Only the empty rooms. They told the boys they must have been mistaken. But the boys shook their heads.

"We know our Elsbeth," said they. "It was our Elsbeth, cryin' 'cause she hadn't no stockin' an' no toys, and we would have given her all ours, only she went out—jus' went out!"

Alack!

The next Christmas I helped with the little festival. It was none of my affair, but I asked to help, and they let me, and when we were all through there were three stockings and three piles of toys, and in the largest one was all the things that I could think of that my dear child would love. I locked the boys' chamber that night, and I slept on the divan in the parlour off the sitting-room. I slept but little, and the night was very still—so windless and white and still that I think I must have heard the slightest noise. Yet I heard none. Had I been in my grave I think my ears would not have remained more unsaluted.

Yet when daylight came and I went to unlock the boys' bed-chamber door, I saw that the stocking and all the treasures which I had bought for my little godchild were gone. There was not a vestige of them remaining!

Of course we told the boys nothing. As for me, after dinner I went home and buried myself once more in my history, and so interested was I that midnight came without my knowing it. I should not have looked up at all, I suppose, to become aware of the time, had it not been for a faint, sweet sound as of a child striking a stringed instrument. It was so delicate and remote that I hardly heard it, but so joyous and tender that I could not but listen, and when I heard it a second time it seemed as if I caught the echo of a child's laugh. At first I was puzzled. Then I remembered the little autoharp I had placed among the other things in that pile of vanished toys. I said aloud:

"Farewell, dear little ghost. Go rest. Rest in joy, dear little ghost. Farewell, farewell."

That was years ago, but there has been silence since. Elsbeth was always an obedient little thing.

Shehens' Houn' Dogs

Edward Berenson, the Washington correspondent for the New York *News*, descended from the sleeping-car at Hardin, Kentucky, and inquired for the stage to Ballington's Gap. But there was, it appeared, no stage. Neither was a conveyance to be hired. The community looked at Berenson and went by on the other side. He had, indeed, as he recollected, with a too confiding candour, registered himself from Washington, and there were reasons in plenty why strangers should not be taken over to Ballington's Gap promiscuously, so to speak, by the neighbours at Hardin. Berenson had come down from Washington with a purpose, however, and he was not to be frustrated. He wished to inquire—politely—why, for four generations, the Shehens and the Babbs had been killing each other. He meant to put the question calmly and in the interest of scientific journalism, but he was quite determined to have it answered. To this end he bought a lank mare for seventy-five dollars—"an th' fixin's thrown in, sah"—and set out upon a red road, bound for the Arcadian distance.

The mountains did not look like the retreat of revengeful clans. They wore, on the contrary, a benevolent aspect. All that was visible was beautiful; and what lay beyond appeared enchanted. The hill-sides flowered with laurel and azalea; the winds met on the heights like elate spirits, united after a too long separation; the sky was so near and so kind that it seemed after all as if the translation of the weary body into something immortal and impregnable to pain were not so mad a dream.

Pleasant streams whispered through the pine woods, and the thrush sang from solitary places.

Berenson had ridden far, and the soft twilight was coming upon him, when he met the first human being since leaving Hardin. It was a slight, sallow, graceful mountaineer with a long rifle flung in the easy hollow of his arm. He emerged suddenly upon Berenson—so suddenly as to disturb the none too sensitive nerves of the mare, who shied incautiously over the edge of the roadway. The two saluted, and Berenson pulled in his nag.

"How far am I from Ballington's Gap, sir?"

"'Bout two mile, sah, if you don't go wrong at th' fawk. Bin to Hardin?"

"Yes—I left the train there."

"Did the folks there send yo' on heah?"

"Well, they let me come," said Berenson with swift divination.

"That theah ole Pap Waddell's hoss yo' all ridin'?"

"Why, I believe it is—or was. It's mine now."

"How much—if it's fair askin'?"

"Seventy-five dollars and the saddle thrown in."

A slow smile illuminated the sallow face—the sort of a smile that dawns when one perceives a joke. The mountaineer drew a long dark plug of tobacco from his pocket.

"D'ye chaw?" he inquired with pensive sweetness.

"I smoke," said Berenson, and offered his pocket case of Havanas. The two lighted up, and the man walked beside the mare as they proceeded.

"We-all bin havin' a good deal of disturbance raound heah, lately," volunteered the mountaineer.

"Yes, so I hear."

"What with the Shehens defendin' theah h'athstones, an th' Babbses raisin' hell, 'twas bad enough—trouble an' to spa-h. An' now th' revinooers—"

"I didn't know they'd been giving you trouble lately."

Berenson did not feel that he ran any risk in identifying his companion with the "blockaders." Loyal mountain sentiment, as

151

he knew, was with the keepers of the stills.

"Yaas, they've bin amongst us ag'in. As I was sayin', all this makes us more inquirin' than polite, sah, an' it's my place to find out the business of them that comes to the gap. As we ah gittin' mighty neah thah this minute, I've got to come to th' p'int." He smiled at Berenson ingratiatingly.

"Well," said Berenson, slipping from his horse and taking his place beside his inquisitor, "you shall have a full and complete answer. I'm a newspaper man, and I've come down here to inquire into the meaning of this feud—this Shehen-Babb difficulty that has been going on down here for the past twenty-five years—or is it longer?"

"I don't know jes' the numbah of yeahs, but it's in the fourth generation, sah. But I don't see why it should consahn outsidahs, sah."

Berenson looked at him with genuine interest. He had a dignity and a grace that were almost distinguished. He bore himself with nonchalance—something as might any clansman, certain of the rights of his position, and firm in his ability to protect his own. He was young—not more than twenty-two. His tan-coloured jeans hung easily upon his lithe and muscular body. His eyes had a kindly expression at moments, but in repose were marked by a certain mournfulness.

"Well," said Berenson, "the newspapers have fallen into the way of thinking that everything is their business. They are probably wrong, but as long as I work for them—and I don't know enough to make my living any other way—I shall act according to their policy. Now, up North, we have become greatly interested in your feud. We have quarrels of our own up there, but they are not inherited quarrels. We don't carry on a fight from the grave to the cradle, and the cradle to the grave. We don't keep on fighting after we've forgotten what the row is about, and we want to know why you do. It strikes us that you have the habits of the old Highlanders, and that these vendettas of yours resemble the old wars of the clans—"

"Waal," interrupted the other, with a philosophical intonation. "We all are Scotch or Irish, mostly."

"That's so!" cried Berenson. "Of course you are! Anyway, I've come down here to get an impartial account of the whole matter, and I want to meet any man—as many men as I can—who will give me the rights of it."

The mountaineer motioned Berenson to stop. He turned to the side of the road, unslung a horn cup from his shoulder, and, stooping, brought it up filled with glistening spring water. He held it out to Berenson with a charming gesture of hospitality. Berenson bowed and accepted it.

"It's good watah," said the other. "I'm fond of watah myself." He spoke as if his taste were rather exotic.

"Waal, I'm powahful glad, Mr.—"

"Berenson—Edward Berenson."

"—Berenson, that yo' bin so squah in tellin' me of yo' business. We don't have many visitahs from ovah yon. 'Bout th' only ones that come heah ah th' revinooers, an' I needn't say, sah, to a man like yo', that they ah not pahticularly welcome. 'Bout fo' yeahs ago a fellow from Mr. Wattehson's papah did come t' these pahts when they was some shootin', an' he took sides with th' Babbs." (A pause.) "He nevah went back." They stopped on a level bit of road to breathe themselves, and Berenson received and returned the whimsical smile of his companion. "But what I like about you," went on the mountaineer, "is that yo' said yo' was goin' to be impahshal. I'm an impahshal man myself, and I think we should all be impahshal. Th' trouble with outsiders is that they ah not impahshal."

"Well, it's a fine thing *to* be," assented Berenson. "You make judges out of stuff like that. Any judges in your family?"

"One, sah."

"Still living?"

"No, sah. Passed away las' yeah."

"What was his name?"

"Loren Shehen, sah."

Berenson's heart performed an acrobatic feat.

"Are you a Shehen, sir?"

"I have that honah, sah. I'm th' last."

"You don't, I'm sure, mean that you are the last survivor?"

"No, sah, I do not. I mean I'm the youngest bohn. Theah's a numbah of us yet on Tulula mountain, sah. Theah's my fathah, an' my two eldah brothahs, an my Uncle Dudley and one son of his, an' my second cousin Edgah—an' theah ah othahs, kinfolk, but not close related. The Judge was with us last yeah, but he was killed, by a hull pahcel of Babbs—a hull yelpin' pack of 'em."

"You've lived here all your life, Mr. Shehen?"

The mountaineer's eyes twinkled.

"Waal, not yit, Mr. Berenson, but I expect to, sah."

Berenson smiled.

"I should think, however, that in spite of the impartial disposition which you say is native to you, Mr. Shehen, that you would have difficulty in dealing with the matter of the feud without some heat."

"No heat at all, sah! You don't git heated when yo' speak of rattlesnakes, do yeh? They ah jest snakes! You kill 'em when yo' kin. Well, Babbs ah th' same. They ah the meanest set of snakes that crawl on theah bellies. That's an impahshal opinion, sah. Yo' kin ask th' next man we meet."

Berenson gave up all effort to keep a sober face. He grinned, then guffawed. He made the rocks ring with his laughter. The mountaineer regarded him indulgently.

"It's a true wohd," he said quietly.

"I haven't had your full name yet," said Berenson, when he got breath again.

"Bill Shehen, sah—young Bill."

"Well, I'm glad I met you, Mr. Shehen! I want to hear your side of the story from beginning to end. Now where can I put up? I want to stay here for some time. It's not alone on account of my paper. I need the rest. I'm tired. I want to talk with all the Shehens I can, and all the Babbs I can."

"Now that's whah yo' make yo' mistake, sah. Yo' cain't talk with both Shehens an' Babbs. If yo' go on to th' Gap with me, and bunk at my place tonight—an' yo' ah welcome, sah—yo've got to 'bide with us. Yo' will be counted a Shehen sympathizah. I don't suppose anyone from th' outside kin ondehstand, sah. I don't expect 'em to do so. I thought about it a plenty. It's jest this: bein' bohn a Shehen, yo' nuss hate fo' th' Babbs with yo' mothah's milk; bein' bohn a Babb, yo' git silly mad evah time yo' see a Shehen. Bein' of one kind, yo' cain't pass the othah kind on th' road; yo' cain't heah of anything they do without a cold feelin' in yo' stomach. When yo' git to fightin' 'em, yo' feel like shoutin' like the niggahs at praise meetin'. I thought it ovah, sah, an' I've about come to the conclusion that it's a disease. Folks call it a feud. Well, I call it a disease—the Shehen-Babb disease."

Berenson put a hand on the man's shoulder.

"Well, then, William Shehen, if you've found that out, why don't you cure yourself? If it's a disease, it's a fatal one! It brings your men to untimely death, and your women to sorrow. Don't set your sons—when you get them—in the way of inheriting the same fearful malady. Get out and get away from it all. Do something besides destroy and make bad whisky. For you do make whisky, I suppose."

"Yaas," said the other gently, "but it ain't so damned bad." His voice had soughing intonations, like the wind in the pines.

"I'll wager you've got a bottle of it in your pocket now," said Berenson.

"Waal!" the wind was never softer on a summer night.

"Well, I've a bottle of the ordinary whisky of commerce. I'll bet mine is the smoother, the nuttier, and altogether the pleasanter."

Three buzzards sitting on the dead branch of a Norway pine received a shock from which they did not recover for several days. They had seen walking along the road two quiet men, one sad mare, and a long thin dog with a lame foot. They suddenly beheld a swift change—a *tableau vivant*. One man stood at the point of the other man's rifle. The mare had jerked away and was backing, with frightened eyes, toward the verge of the steep mountain side. The dog had crouched down as if to get out of the way of trouble.

155

"I believe yo' all ah a damned revinooer aftah all!" said She-hen. He did not raise his voice, but he spoke between closed teeth. His blue gray eyes had become like points of steel. Beren-son, equally tall, in his dark, city clothes, his inappropriate derby above his long, office-bleached face, looked Shehen squarely in the eye.

"I'm not," he said. "I'm just what I told you I was. I haven't a firearm on me. If you shoot, you kill an unarmed man. Besides, you will have made a mistake. The only trouble is, that while I like your jokes, you don't like mine. Up North, when we don't like a man's jokes, we tell him he's an ass; we don't kill him."

The buzzards saw the tableau remain, for an appreciable mo-ment, undisturbed. Then the mountaineer lowered his rifle and flung it back upon his arm. He looked shamefaced. Something like tears came into his embarrassed eyes. Berenson regarded him coldly. The other, meeting the expression, flushed scarlet. Then he shook his fist before Berenson's eyes.

"That's it," he cried. "That's what I say! The life heah makes—fools of us! We ah afeahd of shadows! We have nothin' to show fo' ouah lives! We live to kill—that's it—we live to kill. What has my family done fo' the community? What *is* the community? It's a beautiful country, but what do we do with it? We live like wolves, sah—like wolves. Ain't that how we seem to yo' all?"

He was suddenly no more than a boy. His height seemed, indeed, to have belied him. He looked his passionate inquiry at Berenson, who warmed again into liking.

"Why don't you get out of it all?" demanded Berenson. "Cut it! Quit it! Vamoose! Come where they're doing something—where they're talking about something worth while. Why, you're an intelligent fellow. You've courage. You've had some education, too, haven't you?"

"Dad sent me to Hahdin to the Industrial school; an' I've some books. I take pleasuah in readin', sah."

"I knew it! Well, get out of this place and make a man of yourself."

Shehen said nothing. To the acute disappointment of the

buzzards, the horse was recaptured, the dog recovered, and the two men went on side by side.

The buzzards spread their wings, stretched their necks with a disgusted gesture, and flew away. Silence fell upon the travellers. They were coming to a hamlet. Back from the road, bowered in roses, was a tumble-down house. It was built of logs, and divided in the centre by an open chamber. Three wolf-like dogs ran out to greet Shehen. The mountaineer stopped to welcome them, rubbing his hands over their backs, scratching them behind the ears, and finally lifting one of them up in his arms.

"They seem to be very quiet hounds," said Berenson. "How did you teach them to be so well behaved?"

Berenson's companion regarded him with amusement.

"Thah's reasons, sah, why the Shehens' houn-dogs *hes* to be quiet. We nevah did publish ouah place of residence! But thah's times when they cain't be kep' still, an' that's when one of the clan has bad luck comin' to him. They ah well trained, sah, but they do have theah times of howlin'!"

"And about that time," suggested Berenson, "you want to get your rabbit-foot out."

Bill Shehen nodded.

"If you've got one handy," he agreed. "Fathah an' th' boys have been in a little trouble this week. They ah all away. Come in and spend th' night, sah. I want to talk to yo'."

It was said with the conviction that a refusal was impossible. And, indeed, Berenson considered it so. They put up the horse, and went into the great living room, which ran across one entire side of the house—three bedrooms occupying the other side. Shehen pointed to a crayon picture on the wall—the only picture in the room.

"That's my mothah," he said with a sweet and frank reverence. "She died last yeah." The portrait was a poor one, but it could not conceal the look of fatality in the dead woman's eyes. It was the same look that Berenson had noticed in the eyes of her son. A wave of compassion for both of them swept over him. He was left alone for a moment, and he stood before the crayon, seeing yet not seeing it.

They ate together, and then sat out beneath the hoary hemlocks, and watched the moon rise, scarlet, over the mountain's brow. Berenson felt at ease—at ease with the night, and the place, and the man. The whip-poor-will iterated his foolish call from below them, and almost above their heads the hoot owl cried.

"I can't say but that I'd be willing to get along without those two birds," said Berenson.

"They ah very insistin'," agreed Shehen. "Of co'se I know how to make that hoot owl shet up, but the whip-pooah-will is one too many for me."

"And how can you make the hoot owl hush? By killing it?" Shehen grinned.

"Thah's ways of doin' things up here that you all woulden' take stock in," he ventured.

"Well, I don't know about that. What do you suggest?"

"Yo' all take off youah slippah, sah, an' change the right slippah to the lef' foot an' see what happens."

The industrious owl was in full cry as Berenson bent to obey this extraordinary request. But her mournful gurgle died in her throat.

"She'll shet up now," murmured Shehen, lazily lighting his pipe. And so she did. Not another sound issued from her depressing throat. Berenson made the echoes ring with laughter.

"You don't believe such stuff, man?"

"No-o," pensively murmured the mountaineer. "We don't none of us believe in it! It jes' happens that a-way, that's all. An' I may say, jes' fo' yo' info'mation, thet if yo' haven't on slippahs and it's inconvenient to change youah boots, heatin' a pokah red hot will do jes' as well."

"Thanks," said Berenson, and told of some family superstitions of his own.

But they talked of wiser things, too. Shehen liked books, as he said, and he showed Berenson a catalogue of the year's publications, with the volumes he had purchased or proposed to buy, marked off. He turned to serious matters; was fascinated with popular science, and expressed a wish to have a "star-glass" of his own. He knew the names of the constellations, it appeared, and he called his companion's attention to the colour of the different stars.

"I may be wrong," the Washington man said to the mountaineer that night, "but I think you are wasting yourself here. You ought to have more appreciation of yourself. The only way you can take your own measure is by standing up alongside other men. You're made for happiness and society and some nice girl's love, and good books and a home of your own. I can't think why you've not seen all this for yourself."

The mountaineer reached a hand down to stroke one of the dogs.

"I reckon I've seen it," he said. "But my ole dad is one to have his way. They call him the Ten-Tined Buck of Tulula mountain. It never was much good runnin' counter to him."

"Will you come up to Washington with me if I get his consent? I'll stay here and get acquainted with him, and I'll locate you up there in some way. I tell you, when the chance really offers he'll want you to avail yourself of it. You'll see!"

The sound of the "branch" dripping over the rocks came to their ears. The hermit thrush cast the soft pearls of his melody upon the air. With infinite rustlings, the night settled about them, beneficent as a prayer.

"I mout try it up there," mused the mountaineer. "But I was always a home-keepin' fellow."

Berenson went to bed perplexed. The boy was as innocent and wistful as a girl, outlaw though he confessed himself. Having—inadvertently—finished too quickly and too disastrously his own individual interest in life, Berenson had fallen into a way of deriving vicarious zest by interfering in the lives of others. And, the case of young Bill Shehen seemed to offer a rare opportunity for his benevolent vice.

Three weeks later Berenson went back to Washington. The period of his investigation had not been without adventure—even danger. He had made enemies and friends; he had felt partisanship. He had absorbed something of the point of view of these courteous, murderous, soft-voiced, battle-loving, mountain-whelped, clannish, affectionate, sentimental, law-defying men. He liked them—liked their inconsistencies, their excesses, their barbarism, their hospitality, their piety, and their heathenism. And he carried to Washington with him, as friend and companion, one William Shehen, junior, son of Tulula's "Ten-Tined Buck."

If Shehen was shy, he was also sociable. He had a way with mountains—understood them and answered them—but he had a way with men, too. He was always graceful, and he looked well in the soft gray suit which he got at Berenson's advice, and in the drooping gray felt hat. He carried himself with nonchalance, took long, swinging strides, looked men almost too insistently in the eye, and was rather elaborate in his courtesy. He had, as a part of his indestructible possession, a knowledge of how educated men talked. He had read, and he had remembered. Away from his native environment, he employed something of this knowledge, which came within his literary, but not his actual, experience. The soft tricks of his earth-born, forest-nurtured speech clung to him, but in Washington these were not marked as amazing. His *naïveté* and his gentleness won him friends.

Berenson soon found an office position for him, and he filled it with faithfulness, though his patron never dropped in to see him that he was not distressed at the curious wistfulness in the boy's eyes. He who had known only his own will now submitted, from eight in the morning till half after five in the evening, to the will of others. His days were given up to *minutiæ*, every last particle of which was laid out for him. He had hitherto acted solely on his own initiative, or had followed the rough autocracy of old Bill, his father, the leader of his herd—the Ten-Tined Buck of Tulula Mountain. He was captive now—this wild creature, whose caprices had been his guide. Berenson pitied him, yet expected ultimate happiness for him. Civilization might be rather a stupid escape from barbarism, but after all, when a barbarian got to yearning for civilization, as Shehen had, it seemed best to give it to him.

Shehen went to the Presbyterian church, and he sang so well that the choirmaster requested him to join his baritones, which the young mountaineer did, with unfeigned pleasure. He sang with the open and flexible throat, knew his notes, and was as teachable as an intelligent child. He boarded with a widow who had two daughters, one other boarder and a flower garden. Bill used to work in the garden with the young daughter mornings before he went to the office. Her name was Summer MacDonald. She had had, far back, much the same ancestry as he. Something atavistic stirred in the two of them and gave them sympathies which could not be expressed. Besides, they were both young, they were training roses and weeding mignonette together, and at night they sometimes took a walk in the moonlight. They sang together, too, Summer selecting the songs, which were *adagio* and *andantino*, a trifle sad, and relating to love or religion. She had been going to the Congregational church, but she changed now, and went off every Sunday morning with Shehen, and after a while she got admitted to the choir, too, though her voice was not strong.

Bill liked it, however, the way it was. It flowed along like a pretty "branch" over the mica-starred soil of his mountains. Her face was pale and delicate, and she wore white frocks, and a wide white hat with drooping blue plumes on it. Even in the morning, about her work, she dressed in white, with fetching pink or blue gingham aprons, cut like a child's pinafore, covering them for neatness. With her light braids down her back, she looked like a child. She and Shehen were as happy as they could be. They used, sometimes, when they were walking together in the garden, to catch hold of hands and swing back and forth, out of sheer lightness of heart, and just as little children do. Bill never kissed her, but sometimes, when he was sleeping and the summer wind, perfumed from her garden, blew in upon him, he dreamt that she had kissed him. The caress was as light as thistle down; it had the breath of violets, and it made him blush with happiness.

161

Berenson used to take Shehen around the Capitol, and to the Congressional Library and the Supreme Court Hall. He talked to him, casually, of government, of ideals of law, of the responsibility of a nation. He wished to make him comprehend what a nation meant, and to make clear that individualism need not include anarchy. He gave him a very good notion of how anarchy worked in cities, and he was not surprised to find Bill condemning it utterly. He loathed city crime, too, which seemed to offend him as being squalid and treacherous. Poverty touched him deeply. He could save nothing. He was always helping some one worse situated than himself. Berenson used to wonder if he was coming to have any notion of why the moon-shiners were offenders against the good order of the government; but though Bill's impulses were all on the side of generosity and compassion, he still seemed to lack some comprehension of the real meaning of law. Berenson could never cure him of the habit of going armed. He would, at any time, have been willing to dispense with his uncomfortable collar, or his tie, but his toilet was never complete without his modest Smith and Wesson. The fact that he was, in wearing it, breaking a legal regulation concerned him not at all. It was a point of honor for a Shehen to go armed. That finished it.

"You'll be getting a promotion some of these days, my boy," Berenson said to him. "And then I suppose you and Miss Summer will be setting up for yourselves and making your own flower garden."

Bill settled a spray of heliotrope in his buttonhole. Miss Summer had given it to him from her garden.

"I don't know," he said slowly. "If she knew about Ballington's Gap and the still on Tulula Mountain, and all the Babbs we all had killed, perhaps she wouldn't."

"Tell her the story and see what she says," urged Berenson.

"Yaas," smiled Bill, "eat the mushroom and see if you die!"

As time went on it seemed, however, as if the mountaineer would be likely to eat the mushroom. Berenson used to meet Bill and Miss Summer together, dreamful, on summer nights, and he noticed what seraphic intonation could be given the simple word "we."

"Have you told her yet?" he ventured to ask one day.

"I out with the whole yahn," Bill confessed.

"And what was the effect of it?"

"Waal, it was as if she didn't quite follow me. I reckon she thought I was layin' it on. She said young men liked to play the Othello game—that they wanted to be loved for the dangers they had passed."

"Miss Summer is a student of Shakespeare, then?"

"We've been readin' it togethah," murmured Bill happily.

Berenson could not help priding himself on his man. He felt that fine sense of partnership with the Creator which parents have when they regard a beautiful and virtuous child. Shehen the civilized, the pacific, the bookish, the lover, the citizen, the law-abider, was in part his product. Berenson talked of him at the newspaper office and at the club. People asked to meet him, and Berenson liked nothing better than a Sunday afternoon in Bill's company. Berenson's friends regarded his *protégé* with mingled amusement and affection, and the mountaineer found himself with a circle of surprisingly distinguished acquaintances.

Shehen finally brought word that he had rented a little cottage—a four-roomed affair with a garden plot. He had a charming view, and, with plenty of seeds and saplings from the Agricultural Department, he didn't see why he couldn't be perfectly happy. All he and Miss Summer wished, apparently, was to be together, to have a roof in case of storm or nightfall—and both seemed more or less unlikely in their atmosphere of high noon and sun—and to have a patch of earth to grow perfumed things in. Berenson was delighted. He had not enjoyed life so much for a long time. Having been under the necessity of setting aside the more idyllic department of life, he now regaled himself with his creature's happiness. He had begun to visit the furniture stores with the view to a comprehensive wedding present, and he had set the day when he was to go with the prospective bride to make the selections.

Berenson had his own ideas about how a bride's little drawing-room ought to be furnished. He had, indeed, treasured these ideas for many years. Now, for the first time, he had an opportunity for putting them into execution.

The evening before the day appointed for this agreeable task, Berenson and Bill had dinner together.

"I may be wrong," said the newspaper man, "and I hope I am, my boy, but it strikes me that you're not looking quite so enthusiastic as you should be. Haven't you been sleeping well? You look like a man who's been losing sleep."

"I sleep well enough, but—"

"Yes. Well—"

"But three nights runnin' I've had the oddes' dream!"

"Not a disagreeable dream, I hope! You've enough pleasant things to dream about, I should think."

"Well, yo' might call it a bad dream, an' yo' might not, Mr. Berenson. It's—it's the houn's, yo' know. I heah 'em bahkin' all up the side of Tulula—howlin' an' howlin' like somethin's goin' wrong. It gives me a dreadful honin' fo' home."

"Did you write to your father and brothers that you were to be married?"

"Oh, yes, sah, I wrote to all my kin. I asked 'em to come daown, but I know they won't do that, sah. An' what's moah, the knowledge that I was about to be married would keep 'em from tellin' me if anything *was* goin' wrong."

"Well, I wouldn't worry. Dreams are out of date, you know. You are dreaming because you are nervous, and you're nervous because you are going to be married. That's all there is to that. It's usual under the circumstances."

"I reckon," murmured the mountaineer, "but I suah did heah those houn' dogs!"

He said no more about it, and left Berenson, to make his way to his sweet-heart's house. Berenson, strolling along before going to his rooms, saw the two of them pacing back and forth in the little garden. He heard the low sound of their laughter. They were quite safe in Arcady, he concluded, and went to his bed well pleased with the idyl of his making.

The next morning he awoke with the consciousness of a singularly paternal feeling. He was to meet Miss MacDonald at ten, and nine o'clock found him at his club reading his paper and waiting for his breakfast.

He had unfolded his sheet and was settling back for the enjoyment of it when the door boy entered. He was making for Berenson, and that gentleman of well-arranged habits felt a touch of annoyance.

"A gentleman and lady to see you, sir."

He presented a card. On it were written in the girl's chirography the names of his lovers—just "Bill and Summer" in perfect confidence and unconventionality.

Something was wrong, evidently. Every step that Berenson took toward the little parlour into which they had been shown convinced him that something was very wrong.

It was, indeed, two white and drawn faces that he encountered, and the second glance showed him the girl's face eloquent with appeal and the man's set in stern and obstinate lines.

"For Heaven's sake, what's the trouble?" he broke out, closing the door behind him.

Bill pointed a quivering finger at the paper Berenson had unconsciously retained.

"Have yo' read that, sah?"

"No, I haven't. I was just about to when"—he had shaken the paper out and swept his practised glance over the headings. There, in their ancient and fatal juxtaposition, were the names of Shehen and Babb! Berenson's eye ate up the despatch. The vendetta was on again. Tulula Mountain was a battlefield. Old Bill was slain. So was Loren, his eldest son. So was Dudley, the brother of the elder William. Dudley's two sons and William's second son, Lee, were entrenched in the old Shehen shack. The Babbs held them there, beleaguered—kept them at bay on one side and held off the officers of the law on the other. The Babbs, it appeared, had accessions to their side. The trouble had broken out when some of the contending factions met, during a four days' rain-storm, where much corn whisky was dispensed.

"I'm going back, sah," announced Bill when Berenson lifted his eyes from the page.

"I brought him here to you, sir," cried the girl. "I could do nothing with him! He came an hour ago and told me, and I've pleaded and pleaded."

"You'll go to your death!" broke in Berenson, seizing the mountaineer by the arm. "Or you'll make a murderer of yourself—which will be worse! Don't be a fool! Don't be a lunatic! Your duty's here! Look at that dear little girl. Think what she—"

"They all hev killed my ole dad," muttered Shehen. The vernacular had tangled his tongue again.

"But I say you've no right to leave," protested Berenson, shaking him by the shoulder. "You belong here with that girl. Your honour is involved here, not in that death's hole back in the mountains."

Bill's face did not soften in the least. His eyes were as cruel as bayonets; his face settled in battle lines. He looked taller and his boyhood was gone from him.

"They-all have got Loren, too!" It was as if Berenson's words had not penetrated to his understanding.

"You hear him!" sobbed the girl. "Oh Bill! Bill, dear! I can't give you up. Oh, all our happiness together, Bill—that we planned! And the home, Bill, and all we were going to do for mother and—"

"Great God, man," cried Berenson. "I can't stand the torture of this, if you can! You don't mean to stand there and break that girl's heart, do you?"

"I stand by my kin," said Bill. But he seemed hardly to know what he was saying. He had decided to take the ten o'clock train. He was in a daze; but the one idea persisted. He was going to give the Babbs something to do. If they wanted a target, they should have one. In spirit he was climbing Tulula by those secret paths which he and his clan knew. He saw nothing save the motherly old mountain, with hidden and treacherous foemen

166

in her fastnesses; he heard nothing but the howl of the Shehen "houn' dogs" lamenting the slain.

He would take nothing with him—none of the possessions he had accumulated with frank pride.

"I shan't be needin' much!" he said, a whimsical smile breaking his face for the first time. "I'll fit myself out at Hahdin." He was thinking of his armament.

Summer had given up. After he had unclasped her arms from his neck, she made no further protest. Her pride was wounded to the death. Her world was taken from her—her East, her West, her moon, her sun—as the Gaelic rune has it.

She sank upon a divan, and the tears had dried in her eyes. Berenson went to her.

"There's nothing to be done," he whispered. "I'll call a cab for you. Go home to your mother—to her arms. That's the best place, after all."

She stood up bravely, and he helped her from the room. At the door she turned and gave one backward look. Bill was standing as if turned to stone, but at that glance he threw his long, quivering hands over his face.

"Take her away," he groaned. "Take her away."

So Berenson put her behind the curtained windows of a cab and stood while the vehicle drove down the sunlit street and out of sight.

Then he went back to the mountaineer. He got him to break bread with him. Bill would take little more—but he drained cup after cup of the black coffee. Then they went together to the station. They barely spoke. There was nothing to say. Berenson had not, for years, felt pain so dragging at the throat, the heart, the head, the feet of him. He was clogged and burdened with it, and at the last had only an impatient desire to have the parting over and be through with the sharper misery.

Bill strode before him, unconsciously taking the long, springing lope of other days. His blue eyes were repulsive, Berenson thought. All the sweetness had gone out of his face. Though for a glimpse it returned, when Berenson, in a swift, uncontrollable emotion, embraced him—this consecrated, medieval boy, with doom written large upon him. So they parted. Bill stood on the rear platform of the train, tall, grim, uplifted by his hate even more than he had ever been by love. But after all, as Berenson reflected, love lay fiercely at the core even of his hate. The long train swung around the curve with a mournful wail, and Berenson shuddered. It sounded, for all the world, like "Shehens' houn' dogs" with their prophetic howl.

A Word With the Women

Weekly Column Omaha World-Herald, May 15th, 1896
It seems to be a first draft for the future short story of
Child of the Rain.

Tuesday night was just the night for a ghost. You remember how it rained! All night long the rain fell on the sodden ground. Gusts of desolation seemed to blow about; the darkness was as a palpable melancholy. One shuddered and drew one's baby closer into one's arms for company! The room seemed full of presences, and flutterings of invisible garments moved about, or passing blots of white that might be faces, showed ghastly against the pane for a moment and were gone.

While comfortably housed folk were shivering in their beds, a conductor on one of the Omaha street cars, standing on his drenched platform, saw a little figure sitting at the far end of the car. For a moment he thought the mist of the glass had deceived him, for he had no recollection of having stopped to let any one on, but there was really no mistaking the fact. A little figure sat the end of the car wrapped in an old cloak. Was it boy or girl? The hair hung to the shoulders in unkempt stringiness, and the little cap gave no indication of sex. The ragged overcoat, much too large for the shrunken frame, might have belonged to either a boy or a girl.

The feet were covered with old arctics, from which the soles hung loose. Beside the little figure was a chest of dark wood, with curiously wrought iron hasps. From this depended a stout leathern strap by which it could be carried over the shoulders.

The conductor was strangely fascinated by the tiny shape. The head drooped sadly upon the breast. The thin blue hands lay relaxed upon the lap. The whole attitude was suggestive of hunger, loneliness and fatigue.

"I don't believe I'll collect fare from the poor little thing," he thought to himself. "The kid must need the fare a great deal more than the railway company. It looks starved. If it has a nickel it ought to buy some grub with it."

Then he stood and stared again, for a long time, while the car plunged on in the wet blackness and the rain swished in his face.

"I wonder whether it is a boy or a girl," he said. "It might be either. I'll go in and find out. Perhaps I can help the poor kid along some way."

He was so wrapped in his reverie that he had not noticed where he was and as he opened the door to enter the car turned a corner swiftly and threw the trolley from the wire. For a moment the car was plunged in murk. When the trolley was connected again, the conductor hastened through the open door and toward the further end of the car. Then suddenly, he became aware that the car was empty! There was no sad little figure in the place, no curious box, not even moisture on the seat where the dripping child had been.

The conductor actually looked under the seat before he confessed himself wrong. Then he went to the driver.

"John," he asked, with a little tremble in his voice, "did you let a little kid on with a queer box on his shoulder?"

"Nop," said the driver, wiping his dripping face on his sleeve. "What you talking 'bout? Nobody's got on this trip."

The conductor went back to his own platform and shut the door. The rain grew worse. It fairly deluged him. It was most unlikely that any one would be out on such an hour and so late at night. So he entered the car and stood there, leaning against the door. He was very tired with the long day's work and the wetting, and he nodded for a moment, there on his feet, but as a gust of wind shook the car which almost threw it from the track, he opened his eyes suddenly and caught at a strap to keep himself from falling.

And there, before him, with head sunk on breast, with little blue hands lying relaxed in the lap, with the curious box beside it was the dejected child-figure again. For some reason the chills of the night seemed to have got in the conductor's blood. Then his courage reasserted itself. He made a rush for the child, intending to gather it in his arms, or do anything by which he might convince himself that it was not—but even as he reached out his hands, the trolley slipped on the dripping wire, a thousand bails of blue electricity dripped from above, the tracks turned into white fire, and the little figure was gone!

(N.B. Only the dull need to be told that there is a time for all things. This weather is the time for ghost stories. There are times when this column is devoted to the accurate reporting of events, but that is on different sort of weather from the present. When the sun, the moon, Earth and Uranus stand in a row like boys at school with their toes on the line, one always writes ghost stores!)

The Great Delusion

A Drama in One Act
For four men and five women

<u>CHARACTERS</u>

DR. JOHN FOREST   *scientist and spiritist*
ELEANOR FOREST   *his wife*
HAROLD FOREST   *his son*
SHEILA O'HARA   *Harold's fiancée*
MARGOT GRANT   *Harold's old nurse*
GRAFTON   *the butler*
LADY GRISEL BEATTIE
MRS. GARDEN   *guests at a meeting*
PROFESSOR DEEMER.

<u>TIME:</u>
Two years after the close of the World War. A night in spring.

<u>PLACE:</u>
The study in Dr. Forest's home in England.

Notes on Characters and Costumes
DR. FOREST: He is a man of fifty or sixty, tall, thin, gray, with a clean-shaven, pale face, and dark eyes that look out from under heavy brows, burning with a fanatical fervour. His voice varies between a natural, rather gentle, courteous, quiet, unpretentious way of speaking, to a deep, impressive tone of commanding oratory. He holds himself with a quiet dignity, and bows with deferential reserve in response to the remarks of his admirers. When he speaks of Harold and of his own work, he straightens, seems

taller, and stares off into space, exultant. Throughout the play it is necessary for the character to catch the elusive hint of satisfaction that the doctor feels in the role of comforter that he plays. One cannot call his air exactly smug, and yet, if he were not so grave, he would be smug.

MRS. FOREST: She is a slim, quiet woman, about the doctor's age, with a weary manner. She rouses herself to smile at praise of him, or to anxiously defend the slightest criticism or question of him; the rest of the time she sinks into a weary lassitude. She is gray and quietly dressed in some sombre colour.

GRAFTON: The butler is a small, thin man, quiet white, with a seamed, smooth-shaven face, dressed in the conventional garb of the butler.

MARGOT: She is an elderly lady, with faded blue eyes, gray hair that shows under her white cap, a dark dress with a long, full skirt, relieved with a white kerchief and cuffs. She seems feeble beyond her years, and piteously distressed when she is aroused from her séance.

PROFESSOR DEEMER: He is a square-jawed, dynamic man of forty-five, dressed in well-cut business clothes, wearing glasses on a dark cord. His movements are definite, and his whole air is that of a successful broker or business man, rather than that of a professor.

MRS. GARDEN: She is a little, elderly lady, brightly dressed in a flowered *crêpe*, with a bright hat to match. She wears black velvet around her neck to hold her sagging chin. She is deliberately, intensely, and nervously young and alert. She turns quickly from one of the characters to the other, with nervous, bird-like movements.

LADY BEATTIE: She is a slim, grave woman of forty, with a beautiful, sad face. She is dressed in mourning.

SHEILA: She is a beautiful young girl of twenty with a tender, quiet manner, a gentle, motherly way about her most of the time, as though she had gained control of a deep sorrow, and had become the finer person for it. She is grave, self-contained, and thoroughly poised. Her detachment from the rest of the group at the opening of the play is very deliberate and intentional, and should be got over. She is dressed in a simple, becoming after-noon dress of dark blue or black.

HAROLD FOREST: He is a haggard young man of twenty-five, dressed in a private's uniform. He moves slowly, as though he had been long ill, and his pale, haggard face is the face of a person recovering from serious sickness. His speech is rapid, broken, and rather casual, as though many things had meant too much to him for him to be very definite about them. He speaks often with a weary light in his eyes, and a half smile on his lips.

PROPERTIES
GRAFTON: A large silver tray, with letters.
DR. FOREST: A pencil and a scroll of paper.

STAGE POSITIONS
Up stage means away from the footlights, *down stage* means toward the footlights, and *right* and *left* are used with reference to the actor as he faces the audience. R means *right*, L means *left*, U means *up*, D means *down*, C means *centre*, and these abbreviations are used in combination, as: U R for *up right*, R C for *right centre*, D L C for *down left centre*, etc. One will note that a position designated on the stage refers to a general territory, rather than to a given point.

THE GREAT DELUSION
SCENE: *The study in the Forest home. It is a dignified and beautiful apartment, with panelled walls, French windows, and a lofty fireplace. Against the R wall, well down stage, is a fireplace with a low-burning fire. Above the fireplace, in the R wall, is a door. In the back wall, U R C and U L C, are French windows. R C is a long, carved table with a wing chair back of it. D L C is a small divan. Against the L wall, about C, is a tall clock, ticking. There are wing chairs D L, below the divan, and well D R, by the fireplace. A small table is against the back wall U C, and a pot of incense burns on it. In front of that table, standing so that it faces up stage and slightly to the R, is an easel, which seems*

174

to hold a large oil painting. It is night. The scene is dimly lighted with a low-burning fire, a floor lamp left of the divan, blue moonlight which streams in through the French windows, and, more noticeable than any other light, a strange lavender light which shines on the picture on the easel.]

AT RISE OF CURTAIN: MARGOT, *a quiet Scotch body with cap, kerchief and cuffs, is sitting immovable in the armchair behind the table, facing the audience.* DR. FOREST *is standing* R C. *In the window* U R C, *stands* SHEILA. *Well* D L *are* LADY BEATTIE, MRS. GARDEN, *and* MRS. FOREST. DEEMER *stands* C.]

DEEMER.—It's been most convincing, Dr. Forest. Most convincing. I came here filled with doubt. I leave, a convert.

LADY BEATTIE.—I've no words, Cousin John. No words. You've opened the gates of Heaven to me. If your dear Harold, whom we all mourned, still lives, still remembers, why, so does my boy. So do all the hosts of the departed.

MRS. GARDEN. —Yes, we may go rejoicing from now on. What I've learned in this room during the past year has brought the sunshine flooding back into my life. I took off my mourning as you see, and I've resumed life as if there'd been no sense of loss.

DEEMER.—But, Dr. Forest—is it not—singular—that your medium brings messages from no one but your son—from no one but Captain Forest?

MRS. FOREST.—Ah, you see, Professor Deemer, dear old Margot is so very new to all this sort of thing. At first she was quiet unwilling to try, but when she saw how desperately we wished her to, she consented. She has always been such a quiet body; shy, except with us. Harold was—I mean, is—the core of her heart.

DR. FOREST. Yes—the core of her heart. When she goes questing into the unknown, her spirit speeds straight to Harold. She heeds no one else.

MRS. FOREST.—No one else. I said to her the other day

that we mustn't be selfish. There were others who longed to hear from their friends—even as we long to hear from our boy, but she begged me not to ask any more of her.

LADY BEATTIE.—No, no, I don't suppose we should. It is enough that she has proved they are still living, all those we thought we had lost. Oh, that is quite enough. I say that over and over to myself. What if I have had no direct word from Dick—

MRS. FOREST.—You have had indirect word from him several times, dear Lady Grisel. Several times Harold has referred to him in his writings.

DEEMER.—Sir, you have changed the whole outlook of humanity. You've slain despair.

MRS. GARDEN.—It isn't that what you have done is so unheard of, Dr. Forest. Others have established communications with the dead—

MRS. FOREST.—Oh, not that word; not "dead"!

MRS. GARDEN.—Oh, pardon me! With the departed. But always there seemed some reason to doubt. There other investigators might have been deceived, mightn't they? With you, Dr. Forest, one of the foremost scientific men of the age—there can be no doubt.

DEEMER.—No. No doubt.

[*There is a little moan from* MARGOT, *and all look quickly toward her. For the first time,* SHEILA *moves, and turns from the window.*]

MRS. GARDEN.—She comes out of her trance by herself?

MRS. FOREST.—We never hasten her. We're deeply anxious not to shock her.

[SHEILA *hastens to* MARGOT, *to her right, and puts her arm consolingly around the bent shoulders. There is another shudder and a piteous little moan from* MARGOT, *and* SHEILA *tightens her arm about her.*]

SHEILA.—It's quite all right, Margot, old dear. You're right

176

here at home. This is Sheila, Margot. Do you understand?

DEEMER.—Oh, yes, poor dear. Well, thank you, Dr. Forest, thank you. [*He turns, bows silently to the women, and then turns and goes out quickly U R.*]

MRS. GARDEN.—Thank you, Mrs. Forest, thank you. I can't begin to say how much—Thank you, doctor; it's meant so much. [*She goes out U R.*]

LADY BEATTIE.—Goodnight, Cousin John, and thank you. One should be satisfied. [*She turns slowly, and goes out U R.*]

[SHEILA *has paid no attention through these farewells, but is still bending over* MARGOT, *patting her shoulder, murmuring to her soothingly.*]

DR. FOREST.—That's right, Sheila, my dear, help her back on to our plane. I dare say it seems a dull enough place to her after all she's been seeing. I'm always sorry for her when she has to come back.

SHEILA.—I'm sorry for her, too, sir, but for another reason.

MRS. FOREST.—Hush, hush, Sheila, my dear. I'm sure you have no desire to distress us.

DR. FOREST.—Let the child say what she has to say, Eleanor. Our boy can talk with the angels if he likes, but I'm quite sure if he had his choice, he'd prefer Sheila.

MRS. FOREST.—Don't be impious, John.

[MARGOT, *with a sigh, looking about with a wan smile and stretching out her trembling old hands before her, tries to raise herself slowly to her feet.* SHEILA *helps her rise, pulling the chair back out of her way, and stands for a moment, steadying* MARGOT, *with her arm around her. With a quick catch of her breath,* MARGOT *raises her head and smiles at* SHEILA.]

MARGOT.—I'm richt enough, now, Miss Sheila. Thank 'e for a gude lassie. My Harold's ane lassie. Thank 'e, thank 'e. [SHEILA *turns and watches* MARGOT *go slowly out U R.*]

DR. FOREST.—Now, come here, Harold's ane lassie, and

tell us what it is that troubles your sweet soul. What makes you feel so sorry for Margot?

MRS. FOREST.—Don't be forever questioning Sheila, my dear. Let her have her reticences. You scientists are so—so explorative.

DR. FOREST.—This from you, Eleanor. If it hadn't been for my explorative ways, as you call them, should we have had word from our boy?

MRS. FOREST.—That's true enough, John.

DR. FOREST.—Speak, Sheila.

SHEILA.—You asked, sir, why I was sorry for dear old Margot.

DR. FOREST.—Yes, my dear.

SHEILA.—I'm sorry for her because we make her do something she doesn't wish to do.

DR. FOREST.—Why wouldn't she wish to penetrate beyond the veil that hangs between our boy and ourselves? She is privileged to actually look upon his face. She sees him moving about his new world, at ease, friendly with the great host of other young heroes; smiling, talking, even singing. She said she heard him singing the other day, didn't she, Eleanor?

MRS. FOREST.—Yes, she said she heard him singing.

DR. FOREST.—What grieves you then, Sheila? Isn't she fortunate beyond any of us?

SHEILA.—I hardly know how to say it, sir, but it's as if she weren't satisfied. In her conscience, I mean.

DR. FOREST.—She's honest, Sheila. Never question her honesty.

SHEILA.—No, no. But she seems so jaded, so exhausted, so pitiful. I can't tell why, but she breaks my heart.

DR. FOREST.—The only thing that need break your heart, my child, is to lose Harold.

SHEILA.—But I have lost him! I have lost him!

MRS. FOREST.—How can you say that, Sheila? I must say it seems ungrateful. Why, the written communications alone should satisfy you. Didn't I, myself, see the pencil moving in your hand the other evening? You can't deny that you had direct communication with him.

SHEILA.—Oh, my dear, you know what the message was—something about being happy and our not mourning for him! If Harold could have got word through to me, do you think he would have said that—merely that?

DR. FOREST.—But the words came involuntarily?

SHEILA.—I was the sincere automaton, if that's what you mean, sir. Something—something—[*With a glance toward the* DOCTOR.] perhaps you, unconsciously—moved my hand to write. But do you think there was anything in that message that meant anything to me?

DR. FOREST. You hardly loved him more than his mother and I, my dear, and yet we are contented with the messages he sends us.

[*As* DR. FOREST *speaks, he sits again at the table.* SHEILA, *with a weary shrug, turns back to the window* U R C. GRAFTON, *the butler, enters, bringing a large silver tray covered with letters—dozens of them. He comes down to the left of the table.*]

GRAFTON.—Your mail, sir.

DR. FOREST.—At this hour?

MRS. FOREST.—It's the first time you've been free since the delivery, John. [*She crosses back to the divan and sits down again.*] Sometimes I'm distressed at your lack of privacy. You can hardly call your soul your own.

[GRAFTON *goes quietly out* U R.]

DR. FOREST.—I don't wish to call my soul my own, Eleanor. If there's anything that has comforted me these last few months, it's knowing that the world needs me. [*He rises again, lifting the letters in his hand and dropping them down in a scattered heap on the*

179

table.] You know what these appeals are—all these letters, visits. They're from fellow creatures who have known an unendurable sorrow. They come to me for reassurance, and, thank God, I can give it to them. I doubt if there is a person in the world today who can give so great a boon of healing as I can.

MRS. FOREST.—But if these people wear you out utterly, John, you can't help anyone. Let them read your books. They tell the story.

DR. FOREST.—But people do read them, Eleanor. They've been best sellers for the last two years.

MRS. FOREST.—I know, dear.

DR. FOREST [*moving from behind his desk down in front of the fireplace*].—You know what it cost to build and endow the hospital for insane soldiers; and you know that it was all done with the royalties of these books.

MRS. FOREST.—Yes. That was Harold's service to his comrades. It was he who did it.

DR. FOREST.—But he couldn't have done it alone, Eleanor. Those who have gone require someone on this plane to co-operate with them. He needed us. He needed our love and faith. Yes, and our skill. We summoned him, made him articulate, and we have brought immeasurable comfort to the human race. We have demonstrated a science beyond science. We—

[SHEILA, *who has moved quietly in front of the picture again, to the right of it, sighs as if with fatigued patience, and turns out the light on the picture. Both* DR. FOREST *and* MRS. FOREST *turn Sharply toward her and stand motionless for an instant. Then* SHEILA *looks at* MRS. FOREST *with an apologetic smile.*]

SHEILA.—Oh, Mrs. Forest, forgive me! I should have asked your permission. I shouldn't have turned out the light. But sometimes he seems so tired, smiling and smiling for our sakes.

DR. FOREST.—You are the one who is tired, Sheila. Go to your room and rest. These meetings are hard for you, I know.

SHEILA.—Thank you. I think I'll go to bed. May I say good

night?

DR. FOREST.—So early? I had hoped you would return after a while and help me look over the mail.

SHEILA.—Wouldn't it be just as well for you to wait till morning? You were up at six, and you've been so busy all day.

DR. FOREST.—I've other things to think of than myself, Sheila. Quite other things. [*He moves to the right of the desk.*] This mail, look at it. From London, Calcutta, Lausanne, Christiania, New York—three more from New York. Even from Vancouver. See, Eleanor, one from Vancouver. All asking help, begging for the secret, trying to penetrate to that beautiful place where our slain young warriors have advanced. Turning to me, Eleanor, turning to me from across the world. I must not think of myself. Out of all the world of rulers, priests, philosophers, people are turning to me—

MRS. FOREST [*rises*].—I know, John, I know. You cannot fail them, of course. But if you'll excuse me, I think I'll go to bed. I don't know why it is that I get so very, very weary.

SHEILA.—I'll go with you.

MRS. FOREST.—Oh, thank you, Sheila, but you needn't bother—

SHEILA.—No, no, I'll go, please. Sometimes I'm as lonely as you are.

DR. FOREST.—Lonely, Sheila? How can you be lonely? How can our boy's mother be lonely? Didn't he send word that he was thinking of us constantly? Didn't he cause this portrait of himself to be painted—this living, breathing thing—to comfort us?

SHEILA.—It doesn't seem living and breathing to me. It seems like a shining mist. I can't endure it.

DR. FOREST.—What's come over you, Sheila?

SHEILA.—Common sense! Actuality! They've come over me! I may as well say what I think! I may as well be honest! I don't believe in that picture. I don't believe it was painted by

181

spirits. I think Arnold painted it himself, consciously and deliberately, and lied about it, and sold it to you for a magnificent sum. And I think he laughs at you. I hate him.

DR. FOREST.—Mother, she's tired. You'd better go to bed, both of you, and may Harold speak to you in your dreams. [*He sits at his desk again.*] He comes to me almost nightly in my dreams.

[MRS. FOREST *leans over slowly, and kisses him, looks at him anxiously, and then, with a little sigh, crosses to the door and precedes* SHEILA *out the door* U R. DR. FOREST *sits a moment at his desk, glances toward the portrait, sees it is dark, rises and turns on the electricity. He steps backward to his chair, seats himself, seizes a pencil, and begins to write. There comes a cautious movement, and a shadow against the French window left of the portrait. For a moment the shadow stands against the window, and then moves on to the window* U R C. *The window opens slowly and a young man, sallow faced, haggard, dressed in a worn private's uniform, stands in the window. He makes a movement as though to come forward, then hesitates, steps back, moves out backward through the window, and, with a long look at* DR. FOREST, *closes the window slowly. A pause. Then there comes a sharp knock at the door* R. *It is repeated.* DR. FOREST, *startled by this disturbance, cries out.*]

DR. FOREST.—What! What! What is it, I say? Who?

[*The door* R *opens and* GRAFTON *staggers into the room, frightened, breathless, and pauses left of the desk, leaning on it*].

DR. FOREST.—What is it? Speak!

GRAFTON.—Oh, sir! Oh, sir! I must tell you—

DR. FOREST [*rises slowly*].—A fresh sorrow, Grafton? I am prepared. I am in the care of my God. He will not desert me.

GRAFTON.—Not sorrow, sir, not sorrow. Joy. Joy—Look!

[HAROLD *enters slowly* U R. DR. FOREST *looks at him in amazed delight, and speaks in a glad whisper.*]

DR. FOREST.—A materialization, at last! His very image.

You see it, Graton, don't you? You see it?

GRAFTON.—Oh, sir, don't you hunderstand? It's 'imself. It's Mr. 'Arold, come back, livin' sir; im as was reported dead.

DR. FOREST.—No wonder you think so, Grafton. I'd think so, myself, if I didn't know the truth. I've waited and waited for this, but I never dreamed it would be so wonderful, so real.

HAROLD.—Dad, I'm no ghost. It's Harold.

DR. FOREST.—Grafton, he's speaking!

GRAFTON.—'Course 'e's a-speakin', sir. Why shouldn't 'e? Welcome 'ome, Mr. 'Arold, beggin' your pardon. Welcome 'ome.

HAROLD.—Thank you, Grafton. See, Dad, he knows. He understands I'm real. Oh, Dad, it's good—[*He reaches out his hand to his father.*]

DR. FOREST [*takes* HAROLD'S *hand experimentally and looks at it with scientific detachment*].—Perfect ectoplasm. The emanation of myself, of my own profound desire. [*He drops the boy's hand.*]

HAROLD.—Dad, has it been too much? Shall Grafton call for Mother? It's really Harold, Dad. It's a good joke on us all. I've been lying for months in that hospital you erected in my memory. For months I was there. No mind, no recollection. No consciousness at all for a long time. Then, bit by bit, I began to know I was in the world.

GRAFTON.—Mr. 'Arold!

HAROLD.—You see, they had picked me out of some unspeakable mess. Picked a dozen of us out. Stripped, mostly; disfigured; most of us done for, dead as herrings. Too messy for identification. But I was lucky. They patched me together. By and by I began to remember, but I couldn't get my name. I tell you, I thought till I blubbered like a three-year-old. But it wouldn't come, and then, today, suddenly I knew. Dad, it was as if I'd stopped and picked a needle out of a haysack. Found it after looking for centuries. The needle was my name, and once

I had it, it grew till it was as big as a sword. Yes, sir, it seemed to me like a sword that I was holding up to the sun. I couldn't stop to explain to the hospital people. Didn't want to explain. Only wanted to get home.

GRAFTON.—Of course, poor lad, of course!

HAROLD.—The ward was as quiet as Sunday when I slipped out. No one saw me. Or if they did, thought nothing of it. One more luney wandering around the grounds.

GRAFTON.—Poor boy, poor boy!

HAROLD.—But, of course, I hadn't any notion of where I was, but I looked up—

GRAFTON.—And you recognized it?

HAROLD.—Yes, by George! There was the spire of the old church and the gable of the parish house I've known all my life. I could have shouted. I watched for a chance, and finally, it came. The guards at the gate changed and took their time about it.

GRAFTON.—And you walked out? Good! Good!

HAROLD.—Yes, and no one noticed. And when I got outside, and I looked back at the gate of the hospital, and there it was: "The Harold Forest Memorial Hospital." Dear, dear old Dad. What a joke! [*He reaches out his arm to his father.*]

DR. FOREST [*tremblingly holds him off*].—Grafton, are you there? Are you there still?

GRAFTON.—Yet, I'm 'ere, sir. What can I do for you? Shall I call Mrs. Forest?

DR. FOREST.—No, no, Grafton, not yet.

[*He edges away from* HAROLD, *who is now by the lower right corner of the desk, and seats himself slowly at the desk.* HAROLD *looks at him, puzzled.*]

HAROLD.—But I don't understand, Dad. It's your old boy, all right. Same old sixpence. Not much good yet, perhaps, but bound to come out all right. But no more dead than Grafton or you. Maybe I've changed. Maybe that's the trouble. You'd better call Mother, Grafton. She'd know me, Mother would. [*His eyes fall on the picture. He looks at it, startled.*] What in h—I mean, what on earth—who is it?

GRAFTON.—It's you, sir, beggin' your pardon.

HAROLD.—I should think you would beg my pardon, Grafton. Who did it?

GRAFTON.—Spirits, sir. It's a spirit picture.

[SHEILA *enters* U R *and crosses slowly* D R.]

HAROLD.—Well, of all—

SHEILA.—Sweetheart! I knew it was your voice.

HAROLD.—You're here, Sheila! It hasn't been too long? You haven't forgotten?

SHEILA.—I'm still here. It's been long, oh, so long, but I haven't forgotten.

HAROLD.—Sheila! Sheila!

SHEILA.—But where have you been, dear?

HAROLD.—I haven't known anything, Sheila. It's been like a twisting, turning hell, sweetheart; a place that never stood still. All I could see was faces that weren't real, and battles that were over—and then, out of all the lies and the confusion, *you!*

SHEILA.—See, Father, that's how he talks! I told you those messages weren't from him. I knew he couldn't be so stupid.

DR. FOREST.—But it can't be! After the pain, to have him again—after the loss—the—

HAROLD.—It's been too much for you, Dad. I should have done it all better. I should have waited—seen Sheila—sent her to tell you. Still, I didn't know Sheila was here. I couldn't know for certain. I couldn't be sure of anything except your love and Mother's. I knew that would last.

DR. FOREST.—There's something wrong. Don't you sense it, Sheila? Our boy never talked like this. He kept things to himself. You never could tell what he was thinking.

[HAROLD *looks at his father, bewildered, then turns slowly and crosses* U C *to right of the picture again, and stands looking at it, puzzled. He is too far up stage for the light of the picture to fall on his face.*]

SHEILA.—He was shy with you then, Father. After all, he was just a boy. But he's grown up now, and he is not ashamed to show what he feels.

DR. FOREST [*takes a deep breath, walks with a firm tread up back of the desk and speaks rather sternly*].—Come into the light, sir. You keep your face in the shadow.

[HAROLD *comes down near the picture.*]

DR. FOREST.—Sheila, come here. Look at the difference. Can't you see those faces aren't the same.

HAROLD.—My God, Sheila, doesn't he believe me?

DR. FOREST.—I believe in my son, sir, but not in you. You're someone else. You're someone who knew him. Some poor comrade of his, homeless, tempted by money—

HAROLD.—Sheila, is he mad?

DR. FOREST.—Mad? No. Sane. Too acutely sane for you.

HAROLD.—What do you mean?

DR. FOREST.—I have held communications with my hero son for almost two years. Messages have come to me, come through the barrage of death. I have two volumes of these authentic messages published. Folk come from all parts of this country and from other countries to be present when these message arrive. Even as you entered, I was receiving a message. I'll read it—

HAROLD.—No, if you please. I couldn't quite stand that, I think. You mean, sir, that you don't recognize me, your son?

DR. FOREST.—I tell you, there's no proof that you're my son. These deceptions are common enough. I've heard of them. Why, my son stands high in heaven. He has met the Saviour of the World. He told me so. My boy has stood before the Christ of mankind. They stood together, two "gentlemen unafraid." That's where my boy is, sir, with the highest, doing his perfect work. Our Ambassador to the Court of Heaven.

HAROLD.—Oh, Sheila—Oh, God!

DR. FOREST.—You could make me suffer horribly, sir, but I shall not let you. I have suffered enough—too much. I tell you, I have found peace. No impostor shall take it away from me.

SHEILA [*turns to* GRAFTON].—Call his mother. Let her decide.

DR. FOREST.—He'll work on her. He'll bewilder her.

SHEILA.—Are you afraid to call her?

DR. FOREST.—Why should I be afraid? Have you ever seen me afraid? I'll call—my wife.

[DR. FOREST *turns and goes out* U R *and* GRAFTON *follows him from the room.*]

HAROLD.—Am I mad, Sheila? Is this a nightmare?

SHEILA.—Oh, Harold, you must pity him.

HAROLD.—I'd have pitied him yesterday when he was mourning, but today he has me back.

SHEILA.—But think, Harold. Yesterday you were his proof of immortality. Your father is a famous man—

HAROLD.—Yes, but Dad wouldn't let—

SHEILA.—For one person who knew your father as a great scientist, ten thousand know him as the greatest communicator with the dead. Look at that pile of mail, Harold. That's the third pile that size today. He built a memorial hospital in your honour—

HAROLD.—Yes, I know.

SHEILA.—That hospital was built and endowed with the proceeds from the books filled with your spirit messages. You see?

HAROLD.—I suppose I do. I come back and shatter his

reputation.

SHEILA.—Yes. You give him the lie. You expose him as a dupe.

HAROLD.—But he can't love a reputation more than his own son.

SHEILA.—He loves his faith above all things, and—

HAROLD.—Yes, go on.

SHEILA.—You'd make him the laughing stock of the world.

HAROLD.—But he's my father, and I'm his son.

SHEILA.—You're his dead son.

HAROLD.—But doesn't he love me, Sheila?

SHEILA.—He loves your memory.

HAROLD.—You mean—he never loved me as he loves my memory?

SHEILA.—That's a hard thing to say, Harold, but do we ever prize real things as we do ideals?

HAROLD.—But you, Sheila—

SHEILA.—I never idealised you. I loved you as you were, and I love you as you are.

HAROLD.—Darling—[*He starts to take her in his arms.*]

SHEILA.—No, wait, Harold. There's more I must say. Please try to understand.

HAROLD.—Yes?

SHEILA.—You see, dear, the belief that you were dead and could communicate with the living, was a definite proof of immortality. It was more than that. It proved that the personality survives.

HAROLD.—Yes?

SHEILA.—That's what people want, you see. They yearn to believe that those who are dead remain the same, and your father's books and lectures have brought hope and faith to thousands; to hundreds of thousands, I suppose.

HAROLD.—I see. I feel like a criminal.

SHEILA.—It's grotesque, isn't it? But with your return, those thousands of messages will mean nothing, and thousands of people who have believed will lose their faith again.

HAROLD.—I understand.

[DR. FOREST *enters* U R, *leaning on* GRAFTON'S *arm.*]

SHEILA.—You didn't bring her?

DR. FOREST.—She is sleeping. My wife is sleeping. I couldn't bear to waken her. I couldn't worry her with such a thing. She'd reject you, young man. She'd know you weren't her son, but she'd be tormented the rest of her days with the thought that you might have been her son. I couldn't endure that. I'd die of it. I've suffered enough. No one shall make me suffer any more.

[GRAFTON *helps* DR. FOREST *into his chair back of the desk, and stands anxiously right of him.*]

HAROLD.—No, you shouldn't suffer anymore. I see that. I'll always remember that you really couldn't endure any more.

SHEILA.—What are you saying, Harold?

HAROLD.—I have a confession to make to this gentleman.

SHEILA.—No!

HAROLD.—I am, as he suspected, a fraud. I was seeking, as he said, for a soft place. They said, in our regiment, that his son and I looked like each other. I traded on that. But it wasn't enough resemblance to deceive a father. There is no use in fighting a shining warrior in heaven, is there? I wouldn't try it. Goodbye, Dr. Forest. I'll take myself away, completely, forever. There's only one thing I ask—that you keep all that happened here tonight to yourself. Promise that.

DR. FOREST.—I promise.

HAROLD.—Never speak of it, in any way, to the last day of

your life, to—to—your wife.

DR. FOREST.—Never. I promise.

HAROLD.—Grafton, lift your right hand. I must have your word, too. For the sake of old days, Grafton.

GRAFTON.—My oath, sir. [*Goes out* U R.]

HAROLD.—Goodbye, sir. May you comfort your thousands.

DR. FOREST.—Oh, my boy in heaven, pity me, help me!

HAROLD [*turning to* SHEILA].—Goodbye, Sheila. [*He reaches out his hands hungrily toward her, and then drops them to his sides.*] I've—I've seen you, anyway.

SHEILA.—You don't dare—

HAROLD.—What do you mean?

SHEILA.—You can't say goodbye to me. I'm going with you. You know that perfectly well.

HAROLD.—But, Sheila, I'm penniless. I don't know where I'm going—I don't know what I'll have strength to do.

SHEILA.—I have money and strength.

HAROLD.—Oh, Sheila—

DR. FOREST [*rises, shaking*].—Shame on you, shame on you, Sheila. Can you shame *him* with an imposter?

SHEILA.—We can't argue it, Father. Don't worry, and get comfort wherever you can. Always remember that you're giving happiness to unknown thousands. Hold on to that thought. You're going to need it.

DR. FOREST [*sinks in his chair again*].—Oh, Sheila, do you love me?

SHEILA.—Always.

DR. FOREST.—But you're leaving me. Mother and I will be alone.

SHEILA.—It's your choice, Father. Come, Harold.

[*As she leads* HAROLD U C *behind his father's chair,* SHEILA *pauses with* HAROLD *a moment, and then, with firm gentleness, leads him across the room, and out* U R. DR. FOREST, *rising, takes a step toward the portrait, lifts both hands appealingly, and falls on his knees before it.*]

CURTAIN

LEONAUR
ALSO FROM LEONAUR
AVAILABLE IN SOFTCOVER OR HARDCOVER WITH DUST JACKET

LEONAUR

ALSO FROM LEONAUR
AVAILABLE IN SOFTCOVER OR HARDCOVER WITH DUST JACKET

MR MUKERJI'S GHOSTS *by S. Mukerji*—Supernatural tales from the British Raj period by India's Ghost story collector.

KIPLINGS GHOSTS *by Rudyard Kipling*—Twelve stories of Ghosts, Hauntings, Curses, Werewolves & Magic.

THE COLLECTED SUPERNATURAL AND WEIRD FICTION OF WASHINGTON IRVING: VOLUME 1 *by Washington Irving*—Including one novel 'A History of New York', and nine short stories of the Strange and Unusual.

THE COLLECTED SUPERNATURAL AND WEIRD FICTION OF WASHINGTON IRVING: VOLUME 2 *by Washington Irving*—Including three novelettes 'The Legend of the Sleepy Hollow', 'Dolph Heyliger', 'The Adventure of the Black Fisherman' and thirty-two short stories of the Strange and Unusual.

THE COLLECTED SUPERNATURAL AND WEIRD FICTION OF JOHN KENDRICK BANGS: VOLUME 1 *by John Kendrick Bangs*—Including one novel 'Toppleton's Client or A Spirit in Exile', and ten short stories of the Strange and Unusual.

THE COLLECTED SUPERNATURAL AND WEIRD FICTION OF JOHN KENDRICK BANGS: VOLUME 2 *by John Kendrick Bangs*—Including four novellas 'A House-Boat on the Styx', 'The Pursuit of the House-Boat', 'The Enchanted Typewriter' and 'Mr. Munchausen' of the Strange and Unusual.

THE COLLECTED SUPERNATURAL AND WEIRD FICTION OF JOHN KENDRICK BANGS: VOLUME 3 *by John Kendrick Bangs*—Including twor novellas 'Olympian Nights', 'Roger Camerden: A Strange Story', and ten short stories of the Strange and Unusual.

THE COLLECTED SUPERNATURAL AND WEIRD FICTION OF MARY SHELLEY: VOLUME 1 *by Mary Shelley*—Including one novel 'Frankenstein or the Modern Prometheus', and fourteen short stories of the Strange and Unusual.

THE COLLECTED SUPERNATURAL AND WEIRD FICTION OF MARY SHELLEY: VOLUME 2 *by Mary Shelley*—Including one novel 'The Last Man', and three short stories of the Strange and Unusual.

THE COLLECTED SUPERNATURAL AND WEIRD FICTION OF AMELIA B. EDWARDS *by Amelia B. Edwards*—Contains two novelettes 'Monsieur Maurice', and 'The Discovery of the Treasure Isles', one ballad 'A Legend of Boisguilbert' and seventeen short stories to cill the blood.